Praise for *Air*

2017 YALSA Quick Pick for Reluctant Readers

"With parallels to current political conversations, strong, complex characters whose passionate search for meaning informs their deep motivations, and crackling action, Gattis' YA game is on point."   —ALA *Booklist*

"By blurring the lines between reality and fiction, Ryan Gattis creates a riveting plotline that has the readers thinking deeply at the end of it all."

—Teen Reads

"*Air* is eye-opening and thought provoking, and it expresses the power of voice and action. It's a book that is timely and should be read by teenagers and adults alike."

—Actin' Up with Books

"Life lessons in this novel being portrayed through the eyes of a young man brings personal nostalgia from a period in time most everyone can recognize as how we learn who we are and where our places in life might be. Bringing in many elements of today's world, it is easy to remain connected to characters realistic and probable lives."   —Jagged Edge Reviews

"The action in *Air* is enough to keep a reader reading, yet another reason to be engrossed by this book is the way in which Gattis causes readers to question the true meaning of freedom."
— Gina Hagler

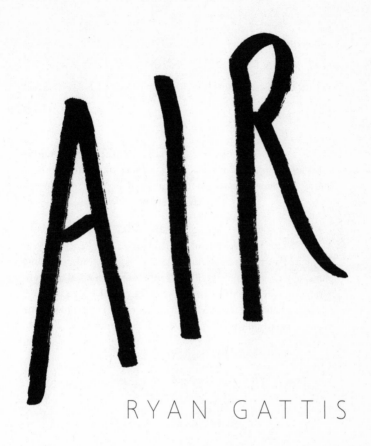

RYAN GATTIS

ADAPTIVE BOOKS

An Imprint of Adaptive Studios
Culver City, CA

Visit us on the web at www.adaptivestudios.com

Library of Congress Cataloging-in-Publication Number:
2015954023

ISBN 978-0-9864484-2-3
pbk B&N ISBN 978-1-945293-29-0
Ebook ISBN 978-0-9964887-2-3

Printed in the USA
Designed by Torborg Davern Design
First paperback edition, 2017

Adaptive Books
Culver City, CA

10 9 8 7 6 5 4 3 2 1

Dedicated to
Mike Raulston
for
never having a filter while
allowing me to see what it means to be grey

TABLE OF CONTENTS

"... there's always an element of crime in freedom."
—RALPH WALDO ELLISON, *INVISIBLE MAN*

1

YOU READY?

Doesn't feel like I could ever get any farther away from Colorado than at the top of the Transamerica Tower, forty stories above Baltimore. I get a weird thought then, standing that high up, feeling the wind: If I die today, my tombstone will have my end date as 2014, and I'm okay with that. Not even a year after my mother's.

I'm peering out onto the city from my perch on the corner, looking down on South Charles and Pratt. To my left is the Inner Harbor. The U.S.S. *Constitution* is sitting there tied to a dock, but I can't see that far. Seeing it and knowing it are two different things.

I'm still not used to being near the sea. I never told anybody this before, but for me, being in a bay, a port, it's like being in the mouth of something that's always looking to chomp down on you, a little like Pinocchio and that whale. Which I guess is just my way of saying I never felt the teeth before. Being grey here is not like being grey back in Colorado Springs. Believe that.

Matter of fact, I never thought about it much until now, but I miss having the mountains on my west at all times. When you come from Colorado, especially the Front Range, that's your compass. You always know where you are. The mountains are your needle. They always show you West. But here, there's nothing but flatness. No way to know if I'm going the right direction.

You got to get altitude to see anything and know for sure.

And forty stories up, it's quieter than you'd think. Sound just doesn't reach up this high. It has *limits*. I've never really thought so much about that word as I have since I was forced to move here. Before, it wasn't something I thought much about, I guess. It wasn't something to challenge and fight with, and get over on. It was just a word.

My hands are shaking now, not like out of control, but like a steady, rhythmic twitch. Feels like I got low-grade electricity going through me. Like I'm plugged in.

It's colder than I thought it'd be for an April day. The Mount Vernon weather station, about twelve blocks from here, said variable wind speed throughout the evening, with gusts up to fourteen miles per hour, and when we heard that, we were like *damn*, but oh well.

Fourteen miles per hour might not sound like a lot, but it's enough to kill us if we catch it wrong. If it blows back off a building and rolls against me, if it swirls, that's it.

But we're past committing to do this now. It's happening. That's it. *No two ways about it*, as Aunt Blue would say.

I'm nervous like kids on the first day of school. I guess that's understandable because I've never jumped off a building before, which means the likelihood of me surviving this is low, maybe even nonexistent.

At least, I think, *at least I'm not in this alone.*

I look across the roof to the corner opposite mine, the one on Pratt and Light Street, and I see Kurtis scramble up onto that ledge.

We're in this together, sure, but we're still missing somebody. What do you call the three musketeers when one of them goes to his rest anyway? You can't call them the two musketeers. Just doesn't sound right.

Man, you don't even know how much I wish Akil was out here with us! If this were anything like before, he'd be watching us from below, ready to orchestrate everything by swooping up and rescuing us the second we put our soles on asphalt. We'd be on the backs of bikes in seconds and just rip, man. We'd feel the wind in our faces as our hearts settled down because sixty miles an hour never had nothing on maximum velocity. That's when it'd sink in what we did.

I miss those times. Kurtis does too even if he'll never say it.

Tonight's different, though. There's no nets. No wires. There's just what we got strapped to our backs, there's just what we're wearing, because this right here is the finale of everything we've ever built up. Every point proved. Every idea we ever had.

No more logos now. No flags. No more websites.

No more videos except what's shot from our heads and from a distance with one of them zoom lenses that looks like the front of a bazooka.

No more anything but this: Sometimes you have to be willing to die to be free.

People that follow us, that actually know what we're about, they get this isn't a stunt. They know this is a finale and a rebirth at the same time. They'll feel it. They know the only reason we've done anything since Akil died is to prove something, to say something important, and this? This is just the exclamation point on all of it, and if it ends up bloody—well, then it ends up bloody.

We wouldn't be the first dead black and grey men in the history of America. And at least we'd have died for a cause. *Our* cause.

Five hundred twenty-nine feet of it. That's only a couple hands shy of fifty-three basketball hoops stacked up end to end.

Through my sneakers I feel the edge of the roof with my toes. I tap it. I feel every muscle in my feet. Every vein. And the electricity is stronger now. I feel it in my shoulders, my cheeks, the tip of my nose.

I look past the convention center, past the elevated concrete walkway that connects it to the hotel across the street, and I think, *There's no way I'm going to make this.* No. Way.

And the weird thing is, I'm cool with that. If I end up pizza on the pavement, then that's what it is.

I'm shivering now. Not because of the cold, though. Because the adrenaline's worked its way through me, as deep as it'll go, and now I just need to go. I need to jump or I never will.

So I look to the other corner of the roof, the one pointing to the harbor on Light and Pratt, and I see Kurtis there, perched on that edge too. He's looking down. Below him, I don't see individual people, but I see a crowd and cars and bright white TV lights for reporters doing live interviews.

They don't even know we're up here. But they will. It's everything we wanted. "Are *you* good?" I'm asking Kurtis as I'm looking at him, but the second it's out of my mouth I realize it's stupid because I know he can't hear me. He's too far away.

And I know he's not good. Not even close.

I look where he's looking and see a perimeter getting set out on Pratt from South Charles to Light Street to keep the people back, to keep cars from going through. I imagine the cops licking their chops at catching us, like some cartoon wolves down there. *Finally.* That's what they must be thinking. After all the trouble we caused, P.O.S.S.E. really did catch up.

It's this moment that Kurtis picks to meet my eye. I can't really tell, but from this distance it looks like he's frowning a little. He looks scared for the first time I've ever seen, so I mouth the words, "You ready?" at him, except I exaggerate so maybe he can see what I mean. I nod my head into it. I put a question mark on the end by putting my hands up.

He gets it.

I see his body sag as he lets all his breath go before nodding, and when he nods, I feel it in my chest like glass breaking inside of me.

Because that means it's time. And it's not like some count-down shit. There's no three-two-one.

It's just *go*.

So I don't even hesitate.

I face the convention center one more time and lean out, spreading my arms behind me as I step off the edge.

Into nothing but air.

2

COLORADO KILLED MY MOTHER

My name used to be Richard Allen Duffy III, and I carried the same name as the man that killed my mother. Now, I know you could be doing a million other things right now besides reading my story, but if you want to know how I ended up jumping off the tallest building in Maryland and not caring if I lived or died, then you should probably hear where I started, because none of this would've happened if my mother was still here.

I was born in San Pedro, California, but I grew up in Colorado Springs, Colorado.

If you don't know about it, it's a city at the foot of Pikes Peak, the same place that Katherine Lee Bates wrote that song about, "America the Beautiful." Mountains that are purple. Plains that are fruited. It wasn't the kind of place where bad things happened. It was the kind of place where if you moved there, you

You felt like you could trust people.

oved there when I was eleven, because we had to. My mother was stationed there at the Army base, Fort Carson. She did civil service, which means she worked for the military but wasn't active duty or anything. She processed medical personnel for them, mainly doctors. A desk job.

She was a single mother. I'd never met my dad but I heard he was in the military. They hadn't been together long, but it was enough time to have four kids. After me is my little brother, Jamar, and then the twins, Randi and Ronni. The reason my name sounds so much whiter than theirs is because my dad named me and my mom named all the rest. I think that's why she changed my name too. Not officially or anything, just with her mouth.

As far back as I can remember, my mother always called me Grey. She spelled it with an *e* and not an *a* because she said it looked more English that way, like it had an extra element of class to it. See, she believed in the power of names. To her, they were like magical spells.

Names aim you at the world, she used to say, and she didn't like me having my dad's name. So she gave me a new one. I think she thought it would change where I was going. That's why I know she didn't mean this new name like anything bad, like a cloudy day, or something unclear. She meant it like something majestic, something proud. Like wolves or whales. I don't know for sure, because she never said that last part to me, but I've thought about it a lot since she died, and I think that's what she was thinking.

The name on my mother's headstone is Sophia Renee Monroe, even though she was Sophia Renee Duffy when she died. My grandpa decided she shouldn't be lying under the name of the man who killed her forever, so he had the engraver put on the name he gave her. Her maiden name. Under that, the headstone has the years of her life too, 1973–2013, and it says BELOVED MOTHER on one line and TAKEN TOO SOON on another below it. My granddad put all that on too. For the funeral he came with my grandmomma and stood in the snow with us as the coffin went in, and they stayed for tea and a wake, and then they had the twins pack up, and they took the girls with them back home to Chicago. Jamar got sent to Texas to live with one of my mom's sisters, Aunt Judy, and my aunt Blue got stuck with me. None of them are Duffys. They're all Monroes because her sisters never got married.

My mother used to say to me, "What do you get when you mix black and white?" She'd answer her own question right after. "Grey, that's what. A new color."

She didn't want to hear any of that *mulatto* nonsense. She had no time for *halfie*, or *half-and-half*, or *Oreo*. She said I was whole. I was both. And I should never think different. I wasn't less than for having a black parent, her, and a white parent, my dad. I was more than, because I had two cultures poured in to make me, and no matter how much people tried to tell me otherwise, I was a new thing. Me even existing was a triumph over racist history somehow, and she said one day everybody would be like me. Shades of grey. All human. But until then, well, I had to fight the good fight.

She was an optimist, my mom. Right up until the end.

The deal that day was the same as any other. I had to pick up my sisters and brother and bring them home because my mom always worked late. So, I'd finish up seventh period at Coronado and then I'd cross Fillmore Street and walk over to Holmes Middle School to pick everybody up. They'd be waiting where they always were, out in the courtyard, doing homework, and I'd thank the vice principal and round them all up. Jamar was the easiest, being in eighth grade, but the twins were always rowdy, always wanting to play tag-this or name-that, so it usually took a few minutes to get them to pack their bags and double-check that they had all their books.

I don't remember anything special about walking home that day. It was just normal, you know? It was just right on North 19th, past Ethereal, and right on Oswego. There were police cars on the block when we got there, which was odd, because it was usually quiet, and a few houses up on the right there was this ambulance parked up over the curb with its lights going in broad daylight. I'll always remember that because I've never seen an ambulance do that before unless the weather was bad and they couldn't help it, but there it was, and that was when it hit me: It was parked in front of our house.

Our screen door with a crisscross grating at the bottom of it had been torn right off the front of the house and was sitting in the middle of the lawn like somebody put an ax through it and just mangled it all to bits.

For no reason right then, Ronni said, "Momma?"

I had a bad feeling in my stomach and I was sweating when I pulled Jamar back behind me right as two cops in blue shirts and navy pants came busting out the wooden fence door that leads to the backyard with a handcuffed man between them.

The feeling I had right as I saw that man's face was hard to describe. I mean, I knew him and I didn't, all at the same time. As he got closer and he put his eyes on me, he stopped struggling. He just kind of stood up between the policemen, almost like he was showing them he was taller than they were, and he looked me right in the eyes and nodded at me.

The chill that worked down my back right then could've frozen over hell.

It was my *dad*, and I knew because he had all the parts I'd seen around me my entire life but never been able to put together into a whole face before.

Tall and white, with eyebrows and a nose like mine. A chin like Jamar's. Eyes like the twins.

I knew it like I knew I was breathing.

Never seen him in my life and now I see him covered in blood, trying not to trip over the screen door as all of three of them walked over it and it creaked.

"You have the right to remain silent," one of the cops was saying. "Anything you say can and will be used against you . . ."

But I wasn't looking at my dad in his bloody shirt anymore. I took a step toward the house and in the open front doorway I saw the bottom of a shoe pointing out toward the yard.

It was my mom's running shoe, the kind she'd wear to work and then switch out in the car.

I could see how the red bottoms were worn white at the heel. I never saw more than that.

A police lady with a kind face and a blazer came out of the house and went stomping through the snow to intercept me, to intercept all of us before we could even think about going inside. By then, Ronni and Randi were crying, but not yet screaming out why, but they would.

It was like they knew before I did. Jamar did too. He had his hand balled up in the back of my coat like he was holding me back, keeping me from going in the house. My little brother, with a grip like a bear, he held me back.

I didn't know it at the time, but the last I ever saw of my mother was the sole of her shoe.

3

WELCOME TO BALLER-MORE

All that happened about six weeks ago. Maybe seven. I lose track of time sometimes. What I do know, though, is that I live in Baltimore with Momma's sister Aunt Blue now. She had to take me or I'd have been a ward of the state, basically an orphan with my dad locked up. That was true of my siblings too. It's probably no surprise, but I didn't want to come here. I wanted to stay in Colorado. Or go to Chicago to be with my grandparents, but the twins got to do that. Everybody was so worried about them. One thing nobody ever tells you when your momma dies is that everybody in the family seems so much more concerned about the girls. I guess that's because people figure they didn't lose just a mother, but a role model for them too. The twins got fawned over by everybody. It was almost an afterthought that Jamar and I would need places to go too. None of us wanted to be split up, but it wasn't up to us. Four kids was too many for anybody, especially older people that already got lives. Truth is, we all got doled out to Momma's family like draft picks, and I was the last one. Mr. Irrelevant. It's not the worst being here, but Aunt Blue has rules. Lots of rules.

When my second morning phone alarm goes off, telling me it's time to head to school, I pack up what little I got into my backpack. A three-ring, a notebook, a couple pens, a pencil— you know, school stuff. I don't have to carry books because they give you two sets at Baltimore Community College High School. You get one for school and one for home. I guess because its kids were getting robbed or something.

I put my momma's sterling silver Honda Valkyrie key chain in my pocket. She used to take it everywhere. She'd plunk it down on the counter whenever she went into her purse to dig for a wallet to pay for fast food, or groceries, or whatever. It never got old seeing people react to a black woman with a biker's key chain. People, especially white people, just looked surprised all the time. Most wouldn't ask why she had it.

Some would. Momma had a pat answer for that. She always said she used to ride a lot before she had us, but after, it was just too dangerous. She had to stop for our sakes. After that she'd hug whichever kid was next to her and laugh a high, musical laugh that always made people smile.

I'm not used to the weight of it yet. It's heavier than you'd think and sticks out. I switch it to my other pocket, the little one meant for change that's kind of hidden on the belt line, and then pull my uniform shirt down over it.

Up to now, Aunt Blue's been driving me to school, because she doesn't want me getting in trouble, but she can't today. She's on a seven-to-seven shift. That's a day shift for nurses, from morning till night.

When she left at about 6:30, she poked her head in and made me promise to keep my head on a swivel—her way of saying to always keep an eye out. When I said I would, she nodded as she said *good*, and the laminated ID card for Johns Hopkins Keswick bounced on her neck.

My aunt's black but she has a reddish tinge to her bobbed hair and freckles. She's shorter than me, but taller than my mother, and harder around the eyes. I can tell she's been scowling most of her life because she's got those lines on her face even when she's got no expression on. I think then that if I ended up a nurse in a Baltimore ER I'd probably scowl a bunch too.

You hang on to you, she said.

It's a weird thing to say. I don't get why she says it and I haven't asked.

I'll see you for dinner and you pay attention at school. I want to hear everything about your day when I get back.

She swept right out the house after that, and the top floor groaned a little as the house settled, almost like it had been holding its breath since she was awake and just then it finally gulped in some air.

I used to love being alone. I don't like it so much anymore. I pick up the phone and call my brother in Texas but I hang up after one ring because it occurs to me how much earlier it is there. It doesn't matter, though.

The phone rings after a few seconds. It's my aunt Judy calling right back.

Stupid caller ID.

"You okay, baby?" She's got sandpaper in her voice.

Great, I think. I woke her. "Yeah, uh, fine, Aunt Judy. I was just calling to talk to Jamar but then I realized what time it was out there and I didn't want to bother you, but I guess I did. Sorry."

"Don't take no guilt on my account." She yawns after that. "Just call back later today. Can you do that, baby?"

"Sure," I say.

"That's good. You have a good day at school now. Study good."

She hangs up before I even say good-bye. When I put the phone back on its cradle, I look at my BMX bike leaned against the wall by the bed. It's sitting on two black garbage bags that Aunt Blue cut open to act as a sheet between the tires and the floor. I guess I just miss our rides sometimes. Me and Jamar used to crank pedals every chance we got. Jumps. Hills. All that. He liked to race. I liked to freestyle.

On the walk to the bus stop my momma's key chain digs into my hip so I switch it to my right side pocket. It's cold out. There's frost on grass and fence planks, but there's no snow. Not yet. The walk goes quick once I figure out 40th Street actually becomes 41st. Right after that I pass a brown-brick shopping center, Green Spring Tower Square, that looks new-ish, but then I hit Falls Road and it's like a different planet.

On my side, there's a Domino's Pizza with two cracked windows and planks over another, but it's still in business. On the other side, though, there's row houses—basically, a long row of houses with no space between them. They all share walls. My aunt says nothing's more Baltimore than row homes with their Cockeysville marble stoops. When she was young, she says people used to clean their stoops with Bon Ami powder and pumice stone. These stoops on Falls are dark at their edges, though. They don't look like they've been cleaned in years. In fact, this whole street actually feels almost like a dividing line, but between black and white, rich and poor, or both, I'm not entirely sure.

Nobody lives that close to the street in Colorado Springs. Everybody lives far enough back to breathe. There's always yard in between, or rocks, or fence. There's always something in between. But here, the houses sit flush to concrete sidewalk like they're hanging their chins out on a chin-up bar. This makes it easy to look in the windows. Most are curtained off by fabric that's been faded by sun. I see in one, though, and it shocks me, because when I look in and see an empty living room—no couch, no TV, no nothing—there's a kid standing over a dirt bike and he's looking straight at me.

I must double-take or something because he smiles at me like he's glad he threw me off. I just shake my head at that and finish walking to the bus stop up Falls Road, and when I look away, down the road toward where the bus will be coming from, I don't give him the satisfaction of another glance.

As I'm standing there, waiting, I hear a group of kids coming up the block before I see them on the other side, five or six in all, walking in a pack and hollering out at anything that takes their interest. An old black man with a grocery bag walking out of the convenience store on the other side of the street gets called Black Santa and they pick at him for a minute, trying to get him to open the bag. They only let him alone when something better walks by: a young mother carrying an infant.

She rounds the corner and tries to speed up to get past them. Her kid's wrapped up against the cold but she's not. Her blouse is cut low and she's wearing a black hoodie half-shrugged off her shoulders. Of course they notice her. They notice her good.

"Hey," one of them says to her, "hey, girl."

She's black like dark chocolate ice cream and her hair is done up in braids. "I'm talking to you, with the kid. You got some titties on you!"

The whole crew laughs at that. He's obviously the leader.

On the other side of that, the young mother just throws words over her shoulder at them: "Don't even try it, little boy."

This causes a chorus of *ooohs* to shoot up from the group. Now, I don't know this town, I don't know these people, but I do know that that right there was all this kid needed. Acknowledgment.

"'Don't even try it.' Ha." The leader talks kind of high-pitched, and when he repeats her, he sounds like an angry parrot. "I don't even care if you're a mother. I'll still stick it in you and make you scream. If I wasn't about to miss my bus, I would too."

She keeps walking, waving a hand high in the air behind her, like, *whatever*, but I'm starting to sweat, because this group is the last thing I need to deal with.

Still, they pass her and cross Falls, heading right for my same bus stop. I turn away and hope I'm not the next target, but they're coming at me like storm clouds, and everything in their way has been getting wet.

So of course it's no surprise when one of them says to me, "Hey!"

I feel my ears get hot, because I know it's less of a greeting and more of a challenge, and even without looking, I know who it is by the voice.

It's the parrot.

I don't even turn around. I just say, "No, thanks," over my shoulder.

I don't know why that came to me, but I know it's stupid. I know it dooms me, and that's clear when Parrot opens up his big fat mouth and says, "What you mean, 'no, thanks'?"

That's when I know it's about to pop off.

4

STAY DOWN

There's really no choice but to run or turn around then. Like an idiot, I turn. I face up to Parrot and see five more kids right behind him. They're younger than me by a year or so, but they're hard in the eyes like they've been doing bad things for years. They're all wearing black T-shirts too. Jeans. Boots or sneakers. They mostly look the same, except for one's chubby, one's got a big head, and Parrot's the tallest. Almost five foot ten.

Almost as tall as me.

He stares at me. "I said, what you mean, 'no, thanks'?"

"Nothing," I say to him. "I just thought you said something else was all. My mind was on something."

"Right. Your mind was on something." He stares at my shirt and picks some information clean off it. "Probly something from that college high school, huh?"

At school, everybody just calls it City, and he either knows that and he's disrespecting, or he's just trying to mess with me. I shrug my shoulders to try to obscure the castle logo but it's way too late for that.

"I mean, you can lie," Parrot says, "but I see you wearing that shirt so. . ."

He doesn't finish the sentence, but he doesn't swing yet either. He's waiting.

The rest of them are looking at me, all five of them, and it looks like they're all making up their minds about my skin. I see it on their faces. They see me way too well. They know I don't fit here and they've got me surrounded. I'm turning a slow circle on the sidewalk so I can always see behind me.

"You ain't black," the chubby one says. "What are you anyways?"

"He's black and something," the big-headed one says. "He's a fucking mixed-breed mutt."

"That true?" Parrot looks like he's got a hold of something important now. His eyes gleam and he repeats what he just heard because that's what parrots do. "You a fucking mixed-breed mutt?"

I'm going to say something—something smart. I swear I am. But when I open my mouth, something hits me on the back of the head and my vision blurs like someone threw the wrong pair of glasses on me. My ears ring as I rock forward but I don't lose my balance. I don't go down. I catch something hard with my ribs, though. With my tailbone. And my knee.

Trying to fight six guys is like trying to fight a hailstorm coming from all directions. Left, right, up, and down.

You're gonna get hit. It's inevitable.

The smartest thing to do is run or cover up, but then again, I've never really been smart. I duck and something whizzes past my ear. I kick out and get nothing but air. I take two shots to the back—one glances off my spine and the other finds my kidney—as I get my legs back under me and swing wild with an elbow. I hear it connect right as I feel it. It's a crack so loud it sounds like a home run jumping off a wooden bat.

I hear somebody hit the pavement and groan.

A voice behind me says, "Goddamn! He clocked Demetrius!"

"Shut up and fight," Parrot says. "Just *get* this motherfucker!"

I'm close enough to him to feel the breath from his words on my cheek as I try to headbutt him and miss. Parrot's got me by the collar and he's pulling my neck down.

Hard. I feel the collar stretching out as I try to pull away.

That's the last thing I remember.

After that, I don't know what happened.

I must've blacked out for a few seconds—I don't know how many, five or ten?—because when I come to, Parrot's standing over me and yelling like he just won a world title in boxing.

"That's right, bitch! Stay down!"

The words drift to me through the ringing in my ears.

I do it, though. I stay down. Not because I want to, but

because I can't move for a second. I got no wind in me. I don't even remember getting hit either, but I got this ache in my jaw that tells that me otherwise. It feels like when I had my wisdom teeth out, when I woke up from the anesthetic.

"Welcome to Baller-more, Mr. No Thanks," Parrot says over me. "You know we'll be seeing you around."

As I'm sitting there blinking and trying to breathe, I see the bus pull up right behind him. The driver appears behind the folding doors and asks Parrot what's wrong with me.

"He fell." Parrot adjusts *my* backpack on his shoulder, the thief. "It's slick out."

The driver looks at me. "You coming or what?"

I shake my head. And he shrugs at me, like it's my fault what happened, before the doors close and the bus pulls away, disappearing up Falls after a bend.

As it's leaving, my breath comes back in an awful rush. I don't even care that it hurts. I'm just so grateful I can breathe again. I take air in. Feels like it's got nails and tacks in it. Like sharp edges are opening up paper cuts in my lungs. I don't care. I gulp it all down.

That's about when I realize I'm laid out on the ice-cold sidewalk, just a few feet from the crosswalk on 41st. I cough up some mucus with blood in it for a good minute before I manage to sit up and look around.

I check my face. My hands. I'm not bleeding that I can tell. My back's throbbing, though. The worst part isn't the pain.

The worst part is that nobody's even looking. Cars keep

going by like they've been going by. Across the street, a woman about Aunt Blue's age walks the opposite sidewalk with headphones in her ears, minding her own business.

I work my jaw and it pops in a way I've never heard it pop before. I know I've got to pick myself up and wipe the slush off my khakis, so I do.

And when I'm up and trying to stand straight, I think to myself, like, *okay, that's how it's about to be in this city.* People beating on you and grabbing your bag? Okay. Trust nobody but yourself. Got it. Lesson learned. Could've been way worse too. I know it. That's why I'm mad, but I'm not crazy mad.

I'm get-even mad. Someday, somehow, it's going down again. Next time, though, I'm swinging first.

I spit more blood, but it's not as much this time. Just a few flecks. And I guess that's a good thing.

I wipe my mouth with the back of my hand and think about how Aunt Blue's got a day off after this, and then is back on day shift for Wednesday. I decide that's a good day to pack a different shirt and change into it before I get on the bus.

That's a good plan forever, really. A good plan for any day I'm on this route, because I'm not about to give somebody an excuse again. Not Parrot, not the six of them, and not anybody else.

I laugh a little when I think about them taking my bag. Like, of course they did.

Why not? The victor gets the spoils. That's how it works.

Around the time I'm breathing almost like normal and the

sky seems to be in its right place, I feel eyes on me. Just turning my head hurts, but I do.

The eyes belong to the kid who was working on his dirt bike in the living room. He's standing out on his stoop, holding a screwdriver in his hand, watching. He doesn't seem sad for me, or interested to see if I'm doing all right. He's just watching, and the front door of his row house is open behind him.

We look at each other for a good minute. Me with a look like, *why the hell didn't you help me?* But that just smashes into his look of straight-up stone and gets nowhere. When he breaks that moment of ours by blinking, I turn away and drag myself back to Aunt Blue's house.

5

FRESH START

I'm in the front door and locking it behind me as I'm trying to feel the difference between the outside air and the inside. Air actually feels different when you're having trouble breathing it. Inside me now, it feels heavier—like it's loaded down with dust or something. I think most people never really notice air until they need it. I guess probably the same thing is true of fish with water. It's just there, moving between in and out so simply, invisible unless it's cold enough to show up as a cloud.

This might sound stupid, but air here is different than back home. It's thicker here. I'm at sea level now and not at 6,000 feet in thin mountain air. There's more humidity here too, because we're practically on the water. Maybe I'm only noticing this now because of all that's happened. Because my ribs are messed up. My kidneys hurt. I'm more aware of everything around me because I hurt. And the air just doesn't feel heavy just inside me, but on my skin too.

Colorado air is cool and dry. My momma used to call it *champagne air* in the wintertime because it'd tickle her nose before it turned her nostril hairs to tiny icicles, and even then, it'd still tickle. Well, that was one reason anyway, but there was another: Sometimes when you run in Rocky Mountain air and you're not used to the elevation, it makes you feel loopy, light-headed. Like champagne, I guess. My momma would know. I wouldn't.

Just thinking of her then hits me funny, and maybe it's because I'm so messed up, but I miss her more than the usual dull pain. Richard Allen Duffy, Jr., made me hate the word *dad*, or *father*, or anything even close. He hadn't been living with us, not for years. The police speculated momma came home from work early that day because Junior contacted her and said he was in the house. He might not have been. He might have just told her that and then attacked through the front.

He'd seen a lot of combat in Iraq, things no one could talk about apparently. Secret things. He had PTSD, they acknowledged that, but they wouldn't release his medical files to us when Aunt Blue petitioned for it. National Security. The only thing that was clear was that he'd had a psychotic break, they said, which meant he used to be normal but then one day, boom, he wasn't anymore.

I might've had to testify and all that but Junior killed himself while in custody.

Nobody really knows how. I thought that only happened in

movies or something. Apparently, it doesn't. When she heard that, my aunt said, "Good. Saves us all a heap of trouble." That's how I got to be an orphan, and why I had to leave Colorado Springs and come to Aunt Blue's, and how I ended up changing my name too.

In honor of my mother, I had my name changed legally to Grey Monroe. No middle name. Just Grey. And a new last name. I didn't want it to be different to the one on my momma's headstone. It just didn't seem right. Grandpa liked that I decided that myself. Doing it was a whole big process, though, especially when you're a minor, and I am, at least for one more year. I'm seventeen now, eighteen this summer. Me, America, and Tom Cruise, all born on the Fourth of July. That was my momma's joke. She was the only one that ever laughed at it too. I owe Aunt Blue for helping me fill out all the name-change paperwork and sign it. I wouldn't be a new me otherwise. *A fresh start*, she called it.

I'm cold and still wet from the ground, so I decide a shower would be good. It's better than trying to figure out how to get to school anyway. My aunt getting home at 7:00 is a long way away, so that should give me enough time to try to fix things. The first step is cleaning up.

I open the laundry closet. It's across from the kitchen and it has these slatted doors that kind of accordion up when you pull the knobs and push them to the sides. I've been doing my own laundry (and Jamar's, and the twins') since I was fourteen. My momma was big on personal responsibility. Right now I'm grateful for that because I don't intend on Aunt Blue knowing I got beaten up today. Or any day, really. And Aunt Blue's not just smart, she *sees* things. She'd notice the stains on the knees of my khakis real quick. So I stain-treat those and throw them in a wash that's already filling up with water.

With that done, my only worry is the missing backpack, and I'm really not sure how I'm gonna explain that away.

I strategize as I dig my old backpack out of my wardrobe and hope Aunt Blue won't notice tomorrow, and then I won't have to say how my other one was stolen. Of course she will, though. That's Aunt Blue. She notices everything. So *when* it happens, not *if,* I'll tell her I like this old blue one better, and not the one she bought for me. She'll ask why and I'll tell her it's because my momma bought it for me, and I feel like that'll be a good conversation-ender if I say it right.

I've got to use the rest of my momma cards well. Aunt Blue's smart and she always asks me how and why questions and I have to work out how I feel about things before I answer. She won't let me glide forever. At some point, she'll call me out.

Which is why I'm more than a little nervous about what happened. Sure, what Parrot and his crew did doesn't show beneath clothes, but she might see it in my eyes. I might flinch away if she touches me. If she figures out what happened, she'll never let me take the bus again. She'll keep driving me and on days she can't, I'll be forced to take a taxi or something, which would make me feel like the biggest burden ever. I just know it. So I make a decision.

I need to take the bus again. I *need* to. But I also need some time and a plan first.

When I shut the door on the washer, I head upstairs to the bathroom.

Before I get in the shower, I check my body in the mirror. I'm real lucky.

Nobody hit me in the face. That would've tipped Aunt Blue off quick. I've got a bump on my head, but it can be explained away. My locker got stuck. I pulled hard and it caught me near the temple. No big deal. The lower right side of my chest, though? The ribs don't look so good there. Red and swollen like there's a golf ball under my skin, that's what it looks like. Ice is not a bad idea for it. I try to see my spine and tailbone, but I never get a good angle even when I turn and crane my neck.

I give up and get under the water. Everything hurts worse in the heat so I turn it down and just try to breathe normal. I try to turn my whole body into a filter for the air. When I inhale, I say to the steam that the good stuff is coming in, healing stuff. When I exhale, I say the bad stuff is going away. The pain. The worry. The fear. My momma taught me that. You're probably sick of hearing that. Too bad.

Saying stuff out loud like this doesn't magically fix anything inside me, but it makes me feel better somehow. At least a little less heavy.

Afterward, I go and lie on my bed. They say you're not supposed to fall asleep if you maybe have a concussion, but I can't help it. I do.

6

ODDS & ENDS

Sometimes when I wake up I think for a few moments that it's all been a dream, that I'm at home in Colorado and my momma's downstairs, *skish-skishing* over the kitchen floor in her slippers, cooking up something, but then I turn my head, and I see the little-kid-style baby duck wallpaper that only goes up to about waist-high and I know that's never going to happen again, so I just sit up, wince, wonder for like the eighty-eighth time since I've been here why that wallpaper is even *in* Aunt Blue's house, and then I look at the clock.

4:38, it says, and it has a little red light on the p.m. side. Damn. My head doesn't hurt or feel fuzzy at all, and I guess that's good since it means I must not have a concussion, but the bad is I slept the whole day away. I do that sometimes now. I'd probably do it a lot more if not for Aunt Blue. In fact, she's why I get up right now.

It's old, this house. From the time before closets, I guess, because my room has a wardrobe instead. I make up my bed, pulling corners tight, because Aunt Blue has rules for me here. I really don't know why Aunt Blue's called Aunt Blue either. My grandmomma named her Deidre and she won't tell me why. It's been like that as long as I can remember, so it just is.

Her rules go like this:

1. I got to make my bed every morning—*without fail*, she said.

2. Since I have to wear a uniform at City, I have to learn how to iron, and when I do, I need to iron for the week. Khakis don't press themselves.

3. I got to go to school. Aunt Blue made a big deal that she got me the chance to sit for an entrance test at City. I passed it too, and that made her happier than I've ever seen her, because according to her there were only three good high schools in this city and no nephew of hers was gonna end up somewhere where he didn't have a chance to make it. I try not to tell her I don't get into school like I used to. How it's hard for me to focus. That would just make her mad, or sad, or both, so I don't say anything about it. I do feel guilty right now, though, not showing up today. She'll most likely get a call on

that, and when she gets it, I don't know what she'll do.

4. I got to do what she calls *supplemental education.* That means I have to read books she sets out for me. I get a month for each one. She's already given me the first one, *Invisible Man.* At first, I thought, *cool, a superhero story,* but it's not like that at all.

5. This last one is the worst one. I have to go to therapy because she thinks I might be running the streets if I don't. But for me that just reminds me how Aunt Blue doesn't really know me. I've never been about that. Still, the idea of letting someone inside my head freaks me out. I don't know that I need that.

That's it for the rules. For now. She said she reserves the right to add new ones if necessary. She looked at me hard when she said that too. And she's not Momma. When she does that, you better know there's consequences. Aunt Blue's old school like that.

Comes from being the oldest sister, I guess, ten years older than my momma. Right now I got a lump in my throat just thinking about what she'll do when she finds out I skipped school today.

When I try doing homework, I sure am grateful my books weren't in that bag. I'm trying to be caught up for tomorrow, so I sit down at the desk in my bedroom and daydream my way through my geometry. (I'm a little behind on math, but I do like it. It's more useful than people think.) I try to read my American history assignment on the Underground Railroad but I keep thinking about how good it would be to punch Parrot in the face. If only there was a way to do it that wouldn't hurt my hand. I imagine him wincing as I swing, or, better yet, him not even seeing it's coming until the last possible moment, and then his eyes get wide, like in horror movies.

I imagine this showdown twenty different ways. Me hitting him before he's ready. Me giving him first swing. Always it ends with me standing over him, victorious. His crew stands around me with their stupid mouths open, like they can't believe I dropped him. And then, something occurs to me.

I might know how to make this a reality.

I turn on the light at the top of the basement stairs and go down, right to where Aunt Blue made me put my bags after I'd emptied them. Next to my duffel is a cardboard box about the size of a television with ODDS & ENDS written on it in Aunt Blue's careful capital letters. I don't know why she keeps the copper-colored ends and joints of pipes in there, but she does. Maybe it's to avoid plumbers charging for replacement pipe, but I'm not sure.

I run my hand through the box and it makes a sound like a broken wind chime. I pick up a piece that's about eight inches long, grip it, and discard it. Not long enough. I find another piece at the bottom. It's almost a foot long, with a wider mouth, and slightly heavier. I hold it in my hand like a baton. On the bottom, it's got some scratchings that look like somebody went at it with heavy-duty sandpaper for a minute. I don't know why anybody'd do that, but it makes the pipe easier to grip, so it's the one I pick. No doubt.

I take it back upstairs to my room and hide it in the wardrobe, lengthwise under three pairs of shoes. I'll have to wait two days to use it because Aunt Blue's off tomorrow and back to work on Wednesday. *I can do that*, I think. I can wait. It'll be worth it. It might even be better with the waiting, more like a real revenge.

I have to stop myself. I mean, I'm mad, I want to do this, I want to hurt them, but that's what scares me. I'm wondering if that makes me a bad person. It makes my face burn a little. I know my momma wouldn't approve of the way I got to do it, but she *would* approve of me standing up for myself, of me making sure these kids don't try this again, every day, from here on out. It's survival.

I go downstairs and scoop up *Invisible Man* before sitting on the couch. Since I missed my own education today, I think, I might as well supplement. It's tough getting into at first. I have to read the first page twice, but then I get going and the prologue part really throws me, like how the narrator just bashes the other dude in before later convincing himself the guy just never saw him. And that reminds me of my own fight, but of how it was the opposite of that. I was almost too visible, what with my uniform getting brought up, and my skin too. I trip on that until the phone rings.

I think about letting the message machine grab it, but since it's past time when I can be home from school, and it might be Aunt Blue, I go pick it up. An automated recording tells me that Grey Monroe was absent from school today, and how if it happens again my parent or guardian will have to make an appointment to come in and speak with an assistant principal.

I hang up with relief taking out some of my soreness. Man, I got lucky on that one. I guess it was my one free pass. I make a promise to myself never to miss school again, and I go right back to the book and read chapter one.

This giant brawl, a battle royal, gets described and it is *awful* with a capital *A*. Young black men, most of them in high school like me, blindfolded and slung at each other like two-fisted pin-balls getting popped by a bunch of plungers.

It sure is worse reading it after you've been thumped too. Somehow, as I was reading, I felt like it had happened to me. It was all I could do to struggle through to the end of the chapter. I was just in shock when I reached the blank space at the end of the page. I mean, I felt like the book had just reached out and shook me. I flip back to check the publication date and it says: 1947, 48, 52, RENEWED 1980. I can't get over how many *n* words it had strung through there, and if it was true of the time for men to talk like that. It turns my stomach to even think about it.

To be honest, I don't even really know what to do with this book. I don't know whether to throw it or hug it. Being in between, being both, I feel in but not of. I feel like a hot piece of gum pulled between shoe and sidewalk.

And I'm sick at the white men in its pages. But that blood's in me too. That's the worst part. I saw my dad between those pages. The white man with blood on his shirt. Momma's blood. And it feels true in the worst way.

I just sit for a while after that. Mostly confused and trying to figure out how I feel.

The sun goes down while I am figuring it. I don't bother getting up and turning any lights on. And when Aunt Blue gets home, bustling through the door with some bags, she asks who the hell I think I am sitting in the dark like that.

7

CONTEXT

One of the bags Aunt Blue has is full of fish from HipHop. She hustles me into the kitchen, turning on lights behind me. That's got to be pure Baltimore, calling a restaurant that. We don't have anything like it back home in the Springs. At the dinner table, I set *Invisible Man* down to help my aunt take the white Styrofoam boxes out of a plastic bag. The insides of them are all steamed-up and dripping as I use a serving fork to get fish and French fries onto plates. Aunt Blue sets out the sides, dividing them into bowls.

When she has scooped the okra and the hush puppies into separate dishes, I say, "Aunt Blue, why'd you give me this book to read?"

She doesn't even look to me. She's finishing spooning cole-slaw into its new bowl. "How far in are you?"

"Through the first chapter."

She makes that *unh-huh* noise again as she settles down across the table from me. It's the noise that can mean any number of things, and right now I don't know which one it is. She nods at the book on the table, though, its cover facing up, glossy under the glow of the hanging lamp.

"I read that my freshman year in college." She brings her nod over to the plate with fried fish piled up on it. "Pass that perch, please."

I do, but I don't say anything to her saying she read it in college because it sounds like she's warming up to tell me more.

Aunt Blue grew up in Chicago, got a scholarship to Morgan State University, graduated, and never left. She did a degree in literature, but to hear her tell it, that wasn't much use in getting a job, so she did a degree in nursing just after.

"It's important you know," she says, "if you don't know it already, that there's a difference between textbooks and art, Grey."

"I know that," I say.

And I must be too quick to answer, because she says, "*Do you?*"

Her questioning me like that, and so fast, makes me feel like I'm not so sure, and that's when I start thinking that maybe I wandered into one of Aunt Blue's smart traps and she's about to spring it on me.

"Has a textbook," she says as her voice go up a little, "*ever* made you feel anything like what you felt when those black boys were blindfolded and smashing into each other while the white men howled?"

I shake my head at that and Aunt Blue *unh-huhs* like she knew all along that textbooks mostly make me yawn, even the ones with pictures.

Aunt Blue crosses her arms like she's teaching, and that's how I know the point is coming.

"Art is ideas *in action*," she says. "Art is feelings felt, and processed, and put in a new way. Ellison's voice rose up when a lot of black people weren't certain how to feel about anything but getting by. And his message to his people was that survival might actually come through resistance, that dignity might actually come through visibility, which means not just being seen, but *acknowledged*—through defining one's self and not letting anybody"—she leans forward fast and the links of her watch *plink* the edge of her plate—"*anybody*, do it for you. Or *to* you."

She stops herself there. She takes up her knife and fork and cuts her fish down the middle. Her utensils scrape as she slices those two long sides of the filet into smaller bits. I know she's just a nurse. She doesn't do surgery or anything. But that's what this looks like. When she's done, she sighs.

"Well, that's my take on it anyway. For better or worse. Wrong or not." She smiles a sad smile and keeps talking, but her eyes are down on her cut-up food. "The world is bigger than me and you, child. You're not the only one with pain. Art gives us context. It can reorder our worlds, but only if we let it. And you ask me why I'm making you read that, well, *that's* why. Art—*real art*, art from sorrow and pain—lets you into other people's worlds. Good art makes you feel. Great art changes how you see the world. And it's in that feeling, and it's in that perspective, that we find out we're not alone and we *can* keep going. Even under the worst of circumstances." She brings her eyes up to me and puts punctuation on the end of her thought by stabbing her fork at the air between us. I think she's going to say something about my momma being dead, but she doesn't. Instead, she says, "Eat your okra, now. Don't let that get cold."

I do as I'm told. I take up a forkful of the slimy little vegetable I've never seemed to mind and get to chewing. I remind myself to look up the word *context* later, because I thought I knew what it meant, but now I'm not so sure.

I feel my blood buzzing in me a little. She's a good speaker, Aunt Blue. She could make a living at it if she wanted to. She's good at making me think.

Right when I'm sure the conversation is over, that I'm supposed to take my lesson and move on, Aunt Blue challenges me. "What would your life look like as art?"

I stop chewing. I don't know the answer to that. Or even if I could answer it.

Not right now anyway. And the more I think about it, I think that sometimes questions just need to be questions, I guess. They're like keys. You need to carry them around with you until you find doors with answers behind them. If my life was a movie, though, probably it would have a scene with me getting beat up in it. But I'd be braver than I was. I would've gone down with more of a fight.

Dinner goes on like this, with me chewing and thinking, and her being quiet.

There are no more challenges. Just the one.

I'm not even mad at Aunt Blue for calling me *child*. That's because I'm thinking about my momma right then, but I'm thinking about her in a different way. I'm thinking about how she's not the only momma that ever died in the world, not even the only one that died in a bad, bad way. And that makes me think about me.

Because if that's true, then I'm not the only son that ever lost one, and then I narrow it down even more. In the whole history of the world, I'm probably not the only grey son, with three siblings, of a single black mother who died like that. There's a lot of people in this world and there have *been* a lot of people in this world. Something like this must have happened before to someone else.

I shiver when that thought hits me. Perspective is a scary thing sometimes. It's big like outer space.

Because if this has happened before, there might be others out there like me somewhere. Other people with pain like I got. And that makes me feel warm behind the ears, and I look across the table at Aunt Blue as she picks up the book and holds it away from her because it's getting harder for her to see up close, and as she's reading the back of it, I think of how hard it must have been to lose a sister.

Maybe it makes me sound like an idiot, but I'd never thought about that before, and I feel a little ashamed that it never occurred to me. I don't know how I'd get on if the twins got hurt and I couldn't see them for Christmases and New Years.

And as I'm wondering what else Aunt Blue lost to make her the way she is, she asks my how my day went. Point blank. Just like that. I talk to her about school, but in a general way. About my classes. She gives me some *unh-huhs* and *that's goods*. When I'm running out of things to say and just kind of blabbering on about the castle building and how tall and old it is, she asks how the bus ride went, and how did I like the walk.

Was I safe?

It doesn't take me but a moment to decide to lie.

8

IT'S A GREY DAY

In the morning, I feel better. Well, better-ish. The air's not as heavy, and I only cough up a little mucus in the shower. I can stand a little more heat under the water this time. I never did ice my ribs—I got too into reading instead—but I guess it didn't do me too much harm because when I check myself in the mirror it looks like the swelling has gone down. A bit anyway. At the door before she takes me to school, Aunt Blue notices my old backpack, and I notice her noticing, but she decides not to say anything. I'm not sure why. Sometimes she gives me slack when I don't always expect it.

The next morning, I feel even better. Aunt Blue doesn't say anything about my old bag again, and Parrot and his crew aren't on the 22 bus when I take it up Falls Road. I don't know if that means their school has a different start time or what. After I think that, I wonder if they're even in school, and if they are, if they even go to class and do homework, because I can't picture it. I really can't. I've tried picturing them with families too, but I can't imagine that either.

For me, school's school. Classes are classes. They blend together. Being the new kid from that state nobody's ever been to but they've all heard of, it's like a sign you wear that keeps people away until you define yourself. I haven't done that yet. People think it's weird my name's Grey. I'm okay with that. I don't need to tell them my life story or anything. I think Aunt Blue thinks I'll settle in once I find a friend to do homework with or a girl to like, but that's not happened yet, and from what I'm seeing, there's not a lot of options for either.

When I get back on the 22 bus right near school, I feel my heart sink because Parrot's not on there. None of them are. I know too. I sit all the way in the back so I can see everybody. I have to sit squished between the cold window and an older Mexican guy with glasses and a shell coat that smells like bubble gum. I almost wanted to tell him that too. Like, hey, not to bother you, but did you know your coat—

The doors open and Parrot gets on the bus. He's got two with him, only three total, and I think this is looking up. They don't notice me at first either. That makes me happier than I can say. They don't notice me because they're being angels, of course, already bothering an old man about wearing house slippers out in February.

I slide my backpack down to my feet from my lap. I cushion

it on the tops of my boots because I'm not about to let my bag sit on the messy floor and get dirty. I unzip the top and put my hand in behind my notebook so that I can root around for the foot of copper pipe that's been digging into my back all day. Guess I'm lucky I go to the one school in Baltimore that doesn't have metal detectors and weapons checks, because I would've been so busted otherwise.

Anyway, I mostly just touch the cold end of the tube to make sure it's there. To reassure myself. And I also tell myself this is for survival. This is so I don't get beat up and robbed whenever I see these idiots. One thing I know is that I sure as hell won't be doing this on the bus.

Still, my stomach's jumping around inside me, reminding me none of this comes without a cost. But I got to pay it now. I got no choice. Bad people don't get to win every day. They've won enough in my life. They don't get to win anything anymore. I grab the tube again and squeeze hard, like I wish I could squeeze my dad's neck if he was still alive.

Outside, it's a grey day. Clouds on top of clouds. *Good*, I think. *It's my day.*

Through the window I see trees growing up funny through sidewalk. I see a block of all liquor stores, corner to corner.

Parrot notices me right before our stop.

"Hey, man," he shouts at me, "so good to see you back on here. Was hoping I'd be seeing you again!"

I believe that.

And I don't shout back or anything, but I do raise my voice

when I say, "That's cool. I *knew* I'd see you again."

He's nodding at me. A slow nod. I can practically see him thinking he and his crew—they're both looking at me now—they're all thinking they're gonna do the same thing to me they did last time. I've been holding the end of the pipe this whole time. The grippy end. It's warm in my palm now. I smile at that.

Parrot thinks it's for him and that's good, because he leans back a little before he says, "Well, cool then."

But it's not cool. He's not smiling when he says it. He definitely means the opposite. Even from rows and rows away, I can see that gleam in his eye again.

And I don't look away. I stare at him. I'm thinking about my dad, this time with blood on his shirt. I think about how much I wish I would've hit him when the police had him cuffed like that. How much I wish I could hit him even now. How I'd punch that man's ghost if I could.

9

VISIBLE MAN

When the bus stops, Parrot and his crew get off first. They're waiting for me on the sidewalk. I step down. There's no slush today. It's just cold and grey. The concrete's clean. I've got my backpack by my side. Its top zipper's unzipped enough to allow my hand in. I'm holding it by the handle meant for loops and coat hooks, itching to put my other hand in and grab the pipe, but not yet.

For a few moments we stand there staring at each other—Parrot up on the nearest stoop, trying to look down on me, his crew standing beside him—as if we've all decided without speaking that nothing starts until the bus is gone, so we wait.

I say, "You see me now?"

"Oh, I see you," he says back.

"Nobody trying to hit me from behind this time."

"I wouldn't have it," he says.

The bus makes a sound like it's burping and sighing at the same time when the doors close, and it pulls to the red light on 41st where it stops and idles.

We all watch it out of the corners of our eyes.

And when that green light goes, when the driver presses the gas down and the bus accelerates, I don't wait for them to make the first move. They already got that the last time.

I put my hand in the backpack, closing my fist around the pipe. I whip the copper out like a sword out of a scabbard. I drop the bag and it falls away. I don't hear it hit the ground. I'm too busy swinging in slow motion.

I hear someone say, "Oh, fuck!"

The kid to my right, with a shaved head like a bumpy plucked turkey, gets his hands up in front of him as I aim for his face.

Behind him, Parrot's eyes go wide. All their eyes do. Just like in those horror movies.

Right before the pipe makes contact with the kid's left arm in an awful clunk-and-crunch. It's like two different sounds meeting in the middle, running into each other and dying off, that's what it sounds like. And after it, the kid brings his arm in like a broken wing, screams bloody murder, and runs off.

They all do.

I'm so shocked I don't even really know what to do. My blood's banging up in my ears as I watch them run down the block. I want to shout something like, *Motherfucker, you come at me again and I'll break all your toes*. But that's not me, not who I am. And maybe it's better I didn't anyway. Maybe it's scarier that way.

I'm worried people're watching so I shove the pipe back in my bag and sling it over my shoulder. As I get to 41st and cross the street on the signal, I keep my head on a swivel like Aunt Blue says. Nobody's looking. Again. Still, I don't need to be waiting around just in case somebody called the cops. I've never done anything crazy like this outside before.

I never really told you how it was when we were little (me, and Jamar, and the twins) and my momma's boyfriend was around. I was ten, almost eleven. He was Army too, like my dad, and he used to thump us pretty good when she wasn't around. He was sick. He used to tell us Momma would leave us if we told. So we didn't. And if I'm any good at hiding that kind of thing, like from Aunt Blue, that's where it comes from. Anyway, when my momma finally found out, we moved to Colorado Springs. We had to, she said, because—

The piercing whine of an engine cuts the air behind me as I'm walking, and I turn to see the dude who watched the day before yesterday weave right through traffic on a motorbike and come straight at me. I stop then.

I sling my backpack down and unzip it. Just in case.

He stops his bike right in front of me and puts his foot up on the curb. The blue sole of his shoe sits flush to it as he leans toward me. He's wearing sneakers. The tops are white.

I don't know what he wants, so I nod at my backpack in my hand and say, "You looking to fight too?"

He smiles at me, this dude. A wide smile. The skin around his eyes even crinkles up as he says, "Me? Naw. Not with you looking to play baseball like that. Where you live anyway?"

I don't want to tell him where, so I point roughly in the direction of Aunt Blue's house, back up 41st. I figure that's safe since he saw me walking that way yesterday.

"That's cool. I live right there." He points at the house we both know he lives in. "We practically neighbors."

I say, "That supposed to mean something? Because it wasn't neighborly to just sit there when I got jumped."

"You talk funny, man." He shrugs his shoulders. Beneath him, the engine of his bike's still going, like he could jet out at any moment. "I don't throw in with just anybody. I had to be sure you weren't no punk."

He looks at me real hard then, like he's either trying to make sure he believes what he just said, or like he's waiting for me to stop him and say that I'm actually a punk and he's got it all wrong.

I don't.

So that's when he nods up at me and says, "I got another bike up the back. Can you ride?"

I didn't expect that.

I need to take a moment and get used to it. *Soak it in*, Aunt Blue would say. I take the biggest breath in I can and push it up and out to the clouds before saying, "Can *I* ride?"

This dude doesn't even know who he's dealing with.

"Yeah, that's what I asked you," he says, and he looks like

he's right about to second-guess himself, which is good because he gets to be at a disadvantage for once.

And I push that too. I don't even answer. I'm dragging it out as I zip up my backpack and start walking toward his row house.

10

THE PARK

Back home in the Springs everybody I knew growing up did BMX. It was the thing for a good long minute. We did it so much, it became a verb. It'd be like:

You gonna BMX that?

Gonna? I BMX'd the hell out of it last week. Caught like two feet of air!

That's what owning a super-light, trick-ready bicycle was about where I'm from.

It was magic. When you're twelve years old, putting two feet of air between you and the ground feels like being a superhero. Feels like you're flying. Like, you're not bound to the earth like other people are. It always made me feel like I could leave this planet whenever I wanted to, and everybody else was just tied to it with shackles they couldn't see. That was what gravity was.

Invisible chains. It's hard not to pity people sometimes when you know they've never had that feeling of breaking that hold, if only for a moment. Two seconds. If that.

The hills behind Holmes Middle School were mostly a summer ride spot, because it's damn near impossible in the snow, and I didn't look at it this way at the time, but it was a blessing. That black ice, and snow pack, and slush frozen up into weird tire-track shapes was actually a good thing because it kept me from riding *there*, but it didn't keep me from riding. That weather made me inventive. Necessity and all that. I *needed* to ride, and that's how I picked up freestyle.

I'd shovel the back patio till the metal scraped concrete. I'd knock the snow off the railroad ties stacked up in the backyard to create two separate levels. There was the patio at ground level, and then above it, three ties high, was soil for a garden my momma never planted in, which was actually a good thing. Because she never noticed if I fell in it and left body prints. I never started small. The ties were almost four feet off the ground, and I pedaled over them whenever I could get away with it. I learned the hard way how to make my bike an extension of me. How to ride a line. How to balance my weight on black plastic pedals. How to hop. How to jump. How to flip, even.

I've separated my right shoulder twice. Broken three fingers. (Left ring, left pinkie, and right middle.) My knees are good, crazily enough. My hips are not. I've hairline-fractured them, but nothing too much worse. I've blacked out a bunch. Maybe ten times. Even with a helmet you can concuss yourself. And I have.

So when I get asked if I can ride, I get offended, even if this guy doesn't know any better. When I ride, I'm me and not-me at the same time. I'm a better me. More confident. Stronger. And even though I start nodding when he asks if I know anything about dirt bikes, he ignores me and tells me anyway.

He gives me a quick run-through. Here's the fuel tank, the foot pegs—explaining obvious stuff before he shows me how to start it.

I get it on the first time.

"Beginner's luck," he says, but then he turns away and gets on his.

The biggest differences between dirt bikes and BMX are size and weight. One's a stripped-down motorcycle with mud flaps, and the other's a bicycle. Apart from the engine instead of pedals, the rest is pretty much the same. Handlebars. Grips. Two tires. A bike is a bike. It's the same general skill set. Still, though, it's a whole different world when you don't have to pump your legs fast to make your own velocity, or when it exists and is there for the taking underneath you, all you got to do is let it rip. Grab that handle and gas it. After that, it's all *go*.

So I do. I'm down the sidewalk and onto the street.

He leads. I follow. When we zip down the hill on 41st, leaving Falls Road behind us, carving up asphalt in our lanes like skiers on hills with that banking back and forth without even needing to talk to each other about who's going where as we make these looping lines with our bikes and bodies that nobody can see but us, and when the houses alongside give way to a little valley, we cross over a bridge and look down on the rush-hour traffic clogging up the I-83, and I know I found my new thing.

I know it.

I can *feel* it.

This is freedom. Pure and simple.

If you know it, you know it. If you don't, you don't.

And for me, it works because nothing else sits on my mind when I'm doing it.

There's only the handlebars and how I steer them. There's only the engine rattling through me, rattling my ribs, and it still hurts where I got hit, but I don't care because winds're swirling all around me as my body cuts right through the air and my jacket sticks flat to my chest and ripples out behind me like the world's tightest parachute. The way the air rushes up to meet me, the way it makes a sound that drowns out the whole world—*this is it*, I think.

This is present and future coming together. I've never ridden a dirt bike before, but I know this is *it*. I feel it spinning around in my stomach, because this is me meeting the me I'm supposed to be. I stand up on my pegs and lean myself forward over the handlebars. I feel Momma's Valkyrie key chain dig into my hip when I sit back down on the seat. I feel her spirit whipping along beside me. Like she's near and floating. Like she's approving of me for doing something she probably always wanted to go back to.

He speeds up and I follow. It's automatic. I'm barely even thinking, just feeling.

He moves. I move.

His bike spits and speeds up. I go to fifty.

And then I go to fifty-five.

I watch the speedometer push a calm needle to the number as we're coming up on a park. I know because it goes green on my left, and the land ripples, and rises, and slopes up as we follow the road and curve around to meet it. Man, riding a fast bike isn't so much like *being* in the middle of a tornado, as it is like being the tornado and everything else just gets out of the way.

So, of course the light stays green for us on Druid Park Drive and we barely even have to slow down as we take the turn wide and right, and the same thing happens again at Greenspring Avenue and even though we're going left, there's an arrow for us, just for us, cheering us on, wanting us to ride up the sloped road and into a park with rolling hills.

All these good things happening in a row, it's like God's saying go out and ride. Everything's just lining up, flowing, as we loop and curve through the park. We pass a lake. Tennis courts. Some sort of model city behind fences. A swimming pool. And we keep going. We pass them again. It feels like being inside a lasso loop while it's swinging. Controlled. Tight.

And I don't even know how long we ride for. I lose track of time.

Zipping through the park, rolling over roads no wider than

a car, going so fast it's like watching trees run beside me and fall away when they can't keep up. It's a race I'm always winning because the world will never be faster than me when I'm riding. The world will always be standing still.

And for that time, I'm not Grey. I'm not a Monroe. Or even whatever's left of a Duffy.

I'm just air.

A tornado.

Spinning as fast as I want.

11

STEALING SPEED

When we're back at his house, and the bikes are put away, and we're standing on the stoop about to say good-bye, he says, "You were crazy out there. Like, a natural."

I nod at his compliment, but I'm focused on something else. While we were riding, my momma's key chain almost worked itself all the way out of my pocket. And that scares the heck out of me, even now, because what if it fell out?

I make myself a promise right then to leave it home next time. I don't want her not to be with me when I ride, but keeping it home safe on a dresser is better than riding, hitting a bump I don't expect, and losing it forever. I'd never forgive myself if that happened.

"You know all that was illegal, though, right?" He says it like he's testing me.

When I don't say anything, when I just put the key chain back in my pocket, as far down as it will go, he says, "You're working your way toward being an outlaw now, like a dirt bike John Dillinger—except we not robbing banks, we stealing speed."

I don't know who John Dillinger is, but I know I need to look it up. Still, I love that phrase of his, *stealing speed*. It lights up my brain. I love how it makes it sound like speed is something to be taken. And maybe the craziest thing is—and really, the only thing that makes me worry is I know Aunt Blue would hate this—but I don't care about it being illegal. I honestly, one-hundred percent don't.

In fact, I like it. Freedom like that shouldn't be against the law. Not in a world where husbands kill wives and split a family up all over the country. That thought flips my guts upside-down and I need something to get my mind off it, so I say, "Hey, what's your name anyway?"

It's crazy how we did all that riding and I never even bothered to ask him. I feel bad about that.

"Akil," he says.

"Spell that for me?"

He says it slow. "*A, k, i, l*. Why you ask?"

"It's how I remember names. I need to see them in my head, and if I can spell them, I imagine them on a piece of paper and it helps."

He shrugs. "Ayight. Whatever."

"Akil what? What's your last name?"

"Williams." He smirks, and I can see he's got a dimple in his right cheek running parallel to a little scar. "You want me to spell that too?"

I laugh. "No. I think I can handle that one."

"That was my ma's last name, not my dad's." He looks down at his shoes like maybe they'll crawl off his feet if he doesn't keep them in check with a glance. "Didn't know him."

Maybe most folks wouldn't've felt Akil using the past tense like he did, but it hit me funny, in a place I don't ever talk about with other people. It felt familiar the way he said it *was my ma's last name*. Almost like I'd heard the tone before, coming out of my own mouth I don't know how many times.

I give him a few seconds before I ask what I want to ask next. Sometimes you need to give people a little space before you tell them you can see them, or see *through* them. You never know how they're gonna react when you show them that.

So I ask it nonchalant. "Something happen to your mother?"

Akil turns and puts a blank look on me that I know he's been practicing for a long time, because I've been practicing mine too. Whenever anybody asks about my momma, I got to set myself first. I got to put up my defenses. I got to figure out how much to say. That's what Akil does too, looking like he's weighing me with his eyes.

And he changes the subject. "Man, you want a Peanut Chew or what?"

It throws me off a little, but I try not to show it fazing me. Besides, I don't even know what that is, so I ask him.

"Man, you so brand-new, you not even out of the factory yet," he says, and laughs before handing me a candy bar. "I got something else for you too."

He disappears into the house and comes out carrying my backpack.

At first I'm kind of stunned, and I don't know what to say, but then it occurs to me to check it. I unzip the pack and rummage my hand around inside. Everything is there. The three-ring, the notebook, both pens, a pencil—all my school stuff.

He says, "Don't worry about them little hoppers neither," he says. "They won't tell on you for doing what you needed to with that pipe."

"Thanks," I finally say.

He doesn't say *you're welcome*. He says, "tomorrow then?"

I'm not sure what he's getting at first, or if he wants me to pay him for getting my backpack back or something. "'Tomorrow then' what?"

And he looks at me, Akil does. He smiles the first genuine smile I've seen on him. A smile that doesn't seem to want anything from me but one thing.

"Riding," he says. "What you think?"

When he laughs right then, that's how I know we're friends. It's quick like a light switch clicking on.

Just like that.

12

NOW WE'RE BROTHERS

It's two and a half weeks of riding almost every day after school—of catching up on homework at midnight when I know Aunt Blue's asleep—before Akil tells me how his mother died. I'm leaning against the light blue counter in his kitchen, right next to the sink. The faucet drip-drops onto the surface of a bowl full with water. A few cereal rings float in there like life preservers. They've ballooned up to twice their normal size.

They look like they're about to pop when he says, "You know what cardiopulmonary disease is?"

I don't, so he explains COPD—chronic obstructive pulmonary disease—to me. How it makes it really hard to breathe because your lungs aren't working properly and how that puts strain on the heart because it needs to work harder to pump blood through the lungs. How you need oxygen treatments, or at least a tank, and how the doctor didn't give his momma none of that. He just let her keep working two jobs. He told me how she died slowly, just months and months of never getting better, always getting worse, and how he cared for her, helping her up and down the stairs, helping her get dressed, until the day he found her in her reclining chair in the living room.

While he's going through this, I look through the entryway and into the empty living room—well, empty expect for two folding chairs and his bike on its kickstand.

"The TV was on," he says, "and my mom, she—uh."

He has to take a moment, so I let him. All I'm thinking is how quick mine was.

How Momma was there one morning and gone one afternoon. I can't really imagine how it must've been for Akil, taking care of his and all, watching her get worse every day.

He's looking at his feet, not me, when his face knots up. Akil has that blue-black, African warrior skin that I wish I had.

"TV's on, and it's on news or something." Akil points in the general direction of the living room with a heavy finger and drops his arm. "She in her chair, reclined back. Eyes open. Worst part was, when I first come in, and it was late, so I thought, 'oh, she just waited up for me,' but you know that wasn't—that wasn't waiting up. I walked over, apologizing for being so late, out with friends for anything and nothing. Was so stupid. I didn't even have a good reason for being out late. I just was. And then I stood in front of her and I could see her eyes open and her chest frozen. Not breathing, nothing."

Akil tenses up where he's standing. I know he's fighting the memory, the strength of it. I feel like he's still seeing that moment when he says, "I couldn't even get the remote out of her hand. That's how long she'd been gone."

The faucet drips louder now. I count twelve of them before he says that's why he had to take everything out of the living room. Every *thing*. The recliner. The TV. The pictures off the walls. The bookcases filled with magazines. (His mother didn't read books but she loved magazines and never threw out a single one.)

"I had to get that stuff out," he says, "you know, so it wouldn't be a dying room." That shit hits me hard. Feels like lightning going off inside my chest and charring me up.

Akil ties everything up for me by saying his dad, who has a whole new family in Virginia since he left them, sued the doctor for malpractice. It never went to trial. The doctor settled. They got more than enough to buy the rest of the house Akil's mom had. Akil was seventeen when she died and eighteen by the time the case settled. He hadn't really been going to school anyway, so his dad gave him enough for trade school (to be a mechanic someday) and kept the rest. That was how Akil was living on his own. In a two-story row home. With a living room for his bikes.

I don't know much. But I know when someone shares a story like that, and you connect with it, you got to share yours too. It's like a trade. Like, they just built an invisible bridge from their side to where you are, but they can only go halfway before hanging in the air. You got to build the other half and meet in the middle.

We were friends quick. All it took was riding and getting a backpack back for that. But now, knowing about his mom, and him knowing about my momma too, now we're brothers. We both know it, but we don't need to say anything about it. It just is.

"I got to show you something," he says to me. "Come on."

He pushes off the counter and heads out of the kitchen. I follow into the living room, seeing it differently now, trying not to think about where it happened.

Upstairs, Akil has a computer in his room that's so much nicer than Aunt Blue's.

The monitor's flat, bigger than a TV almost, and when it hums on, a colorful desktop pushes forward from the black.

Akil clicks the browser and it shoots out, taking over everything. It's on a finance page and it's got a list of what looks like stock signs and numbers all laid out on it. We just started learning about this stuff in econ.

Surprised, I say, "You trade stocks?"

"Money don't last forever unless you put it to work," he says back. "Market crash in oh-eight was the best thing to happen to anybody who didn't have stocks in the first place. I got to buy up good companies for cheap and now I'm holding on to the great and selling the good off slow. How else you think I'm living on my own? Buying food? Keeping the lights on?"

I get a whole new respect for Akil then. He's not just a survivor. He's doing it with his brain.

He shrugs. "But that's not what I'm trying to show you anyhow."

Akil switches browser tabs to a YouTube page with a paused video. I read the title and I can tell it's something about riding and Baltimore but that's about it.

I say, "What is it?"

"Just watch," Akil says, and presses PLAY.

A guy rides into the picture. Akil full-screens it right as the dude leans back on his bike, riding on one wheel, as balanced as balanced can be, putting his front wheel almost straight up in the air.

My jaw must've dropped because Akil says, "You trying to catch flies with that?"

He laughs when I tear my eyes away from the screen to look at him doing his perfect impression of my face when I first looked. Eyes wide. Mouth open. In it completely.

I hit him in the shoulder and turn back to the screen.

This guy rides like LeBron drives the lane and dunks. I don't even like LeBron but you've got to give credit where it's due. When he's on, the guy has power, control, and effortlessness all at the same time. Which is exactly what this guy has. All of it.

My mouth is dry when I say, "What's his name?"

"Kurtis."

"He have a last name?"

"Not that I know. He probly hides it. Safer that way." I nod.

When we're done watching, we watch it again, and then we try a link and watch that one, and then another. It takes me about six before it hits me that this is a way to be seen. And not just seen, *respected*.

I want it immediately. Badly.

Man, watching this guy—it's like nothing in life that BMX and dirt bikes have ever been for me before, but this? It feels like it got shot right at me. This place, these videos? They're like arrows coming at me, hitting me deep. I know this life is for me. I feel it in my ribs. I know it like I know breathing. I need to do *that*. I need to be in that place where road lanes don't matter. I need to test limits, take it to the edge.

And that scares me too, because I know Aunt Blue wouldn't approve. No way. No how. But on that screen I'm seeing the me I want to be. And I know I can do it. Actually, I know I have to. Put it that way.

I say, "How do we get a camera?"

Akil laughs, opens a drawer, and holds a digital video camera up to my face. A good one. I give him a look with a nod like, *how did you get this?*

"Sold some AIG," he says.

I don't even know what that is, but I'm still impressed. "You got to teach me about that stuff someday, after we make some videos, though."

Akil nods at that. "Deal."

Sharing videos, that's democracy right there.

People watching it, liking it, subscribing to it. It's like getting elected to a whole new realm. It's a way to be somebody, to be the president of something—in as long as it takes for people to click, watch, and share, you're elected and important and if you got something to say, now you got a whole grip of people to say it to. It's a big box to stand on, and you don't even have to shout. You just have to keep posting.

13

MISCHIEF

The first time I ever sneak out of Aunt Blue's house, I don't really have to sneak all that much because she's not even here. She went to the hospital for an overnight shift, 11 p.m. to 7 a.m. That's rough on her, but I'm grateful for it. It gives me time to do what I want. So, I said my goodnights and looked her in the eye (because it's one of those rules) right before she headed out, but then, instead of going to bed, I got dressed. Normally, I'd wait for the knock on the door, but I don't even have to do that.

I hear Akil's bike coming up the street, so I put *Invisible Man* down and go to the curb outside. I've been hacking away at that book, here and there. I can only seem to read it in bursts. I have to read a chapter, feel heavy, and put the book down so I can think on it. I'm on chapter five now, but that's mostly from skipping parts when it gets slow. I need to hurry up and finish it. Aunt Blue will be wanting to have a talk about it soon, and then give me a new one to read. Hopefully one not as long.

My street's quiet. Across the way is a tree swaying, one of the kinds my aunt calls *weepy-looking.* I don't know what type it is exactly, but it does hang down like a broken chandelier on a stick. There's salt in the air tonight. I can smell the ocean. I can't always, but sometimes when the wind is right, it hits me and reminds me how close I am to it, even though I never go see it.

I've got my jacket on but my hood down. It's been raining mostly. Night temps in the low fifties for about a week. It's a spring that can't seem to keep itself from crying. I see mist in the yellow streetlight halos, but that's about it. The streets are mirrors, but not too slick. It'll be good to ride in it. Even without a helmet, it'll be fine.

Nobody who does what we do in B-more wears one. You do that, you can't be seen. You can't be seen, you can't be known.

And everybody wants to be known. Everybody wants to be Kurtis. Even us.

I see Akil's cyclops-looking headlight coming up my block and lean an elbow on the mailbox as he rolls right up to the curb and slows down, doesn't even stop, and I have to hop and swing up onto his bike behind him. I press my chest to his upper back and put my hands behind me, grabbing the handles that jut behind the seat.

He doesn't ask if I'm on. He knows by the way I anchor

myself into the seat. So he gasses it. The bike leaps under us and my stomach goes with it.

I turn my head and watch Aunt Blue's house go, half of it flat in the yellow streetlamp, half hidden in the dark. She didn't ask what I was up to tonight. She just assumed I'd be at home sleeping. So it's not like I'm lying exactly, but I'm definitely not telling the truth. It's been like that for a while now and if not for her constantly changing schedule, I'm sure she'd be all over me. I bought myself some time with the midterm grades, though.

Four A's and two B's. She liked that. I'm thinking of her face when she opened it as we pull up in front of Akil's. How proud it looked. How happy she was for me.

And that's when I knew my progress was how I'm paying her back for what she's doing for me. That made me feel bad. Because I'm into a rhythm now, and school isn't hard. Never was. But I'm beginning to wonder what else there is for me. And it's these bikes that have got me started on it.

"We here," Akil says, and that's the signal for me to put my legs out either side and push myself to standing, so I do.

Akil turns his bike off and the engine dies. Always after a ride, even a short one, there's this feeling that's hard to describe. It's like you've been shaking, but you've been shaking for long enough that it starts seeming normal, and your body adjusts to it. It's like living inside a cat's purr. It's happy like that. And after you stop, when it's just you and the ground, it feels like you're missing something. It's lonely almost.

Akil kicks the stand on his bike, pulls his keys, and I follow him into the house to roll his other bike out. It always takes two of us to get it down the stairs, to be safe with it anyway. He can see I've been thinking things, though, and sometimes he lets me be, and other times he tries to break me out of it.

Tonight must be the second one, because when we're out the door he says, "You know why I first talked to you?"

It occurs to me right then that I don't. I guess I'd always assumed it was because of how I swung that copper pipe, because of how I stood up for myself.

"You mean how you let me get jumped and didn't say any-thing, and then after I hit some idiot with a pipe, you rode over? Like that time?"

He eyes me. I eye him back. We've never been over this. It's just been that-thing-that-happened. And neither one of us is too good with the past. We tend to just let it sit. It's hard enough trying to live otherwise. It's hard enough keeping going.

"You still mad I didn't help you that first day?" He crosses his arms at me.

"Not mad," I say, which is sort of a lie. I still feel a little burning in my stomach when I think about it sometimes. "I guess I just wondered why."

Akil sniffs the kind of sniff that means something like, *What, I wasn't clear enough the first time?*

"I wanted to see if you were a punk or not was all. I wanted," he says, "to see how you'd handle yourself. What you'd do about it."

"So you watched me fall."

"You bet your ass I watched you fall! You know why? Cause everyone falls. I didn't want to see that, but I wanted to see what happened after it. See, cause, *falling* don't make you a punk. It's the *not-getting-up* that makes you a punk. And that can be tough to tell sometimes, right? Cause someone can physically get up and walk off, but in their heart they're still knocked down. I thought that was you too. When you didn't come back the next day, I thought, well, that's him done then."

When Akil's animated like this, his Baltimore comes out in his *oo* sounds. At first I couldn't hear the local accent, but I hear it in my aunt's voice now, here and there, and I definitely hear it when Akil says *you* and *too*.

I shrug. "Yeah, well, my aunt was off-shift the next day. She drove me to school."

"See, I didn't know that. I jumped at a conclusion, but when I saw them kids I told them where to bring your backpack, and maybe I'd let them see my bike. I was gonna give it back to you if ever I saw you again, and if I didn't, it was mine to keep. That felt fair to me."

This would probably be a good place to interrupt or say something, but I just want to hear the rest.

"But then I saw you the next day," he says, "doing what you needed to do. Getting back on that bus. And I could just tell looking at you that you'd been thinking about it. Being smart. Strategizing. You'd actually been looking forward to it—shit. That's when I knew. See, the real people, the real riders, come back and do what they have to. That's how you know they real."

It took him a long time to come around to it, but I know Akil's giving me the highest compliment he can give.

And then he goes and ruins it by saying, "Oh, and besides, when you told me where you lived at, I thought you were rich, living over here. And I thought that might be useful someday. Can always use new investment."

He laughs, but I know there's some truth in there. Akil never lies about anything.

He might be quiet sometimes. He might never answer your questions, but dude never lies. Not even once. He's as straight-up as anybody I ever met.

I say, "So has it been useful?"

He nods up at me like, *I got an answer to that but I'm not sharing it with you*, and then he smiles to let me know he's just messing with me. But there's something else in his grin too. *Mischief*, my momma would've said. But to me it just looks like fun.

He says, "You ever been downtown?"

"With my aunt some Sundays. Why?"

"Yeah, but you ever been to the far side of the Inner Harbor?"

His smile's starting to make me nervous because it hasn't stopped. Just stays stuck on his face. He's scheming—or something.

And that makes me wary. "What's over there?"

"You'll see." That's all Akil says before he straddles his bike, gets it going, and takes off down Falls.

I don't really have a choice. If I want to find out, I have to go too. So I rip after him, that's what I do.

14

OUT OF NOWHERE

It's a Wednesday March night. Nothing much going on. Most people, good people, are in beds asleep. Or they're working. They sure as hell aren't out riding. In general, there's no worse time to ride. Most riders do Druid Hill Park on Sundays so there's safety in numbers. Discourages the cops that way. Keeps them honest when it's not just people on bikes but people standing on curbs, watching, recording with their phones and whatnot. Witnesses, that's what.

Tonight it's just us two, though, so we go the speed limit. We keep it close. We don't do anything but stay in our lane. I was hungry before, but not now. Smell enough exhaust and you get a sting in the front of your face. Around your nose. Around the eyes. I do anyway. The taste just kind of sinks into my tongue and makes me feel a little sick. Burnt lint traps in dryers. It tastes like that smell to me. That's why I'd rather ride side-by-side like we're a car. He just happens to have two wheels, and I've got the other two. Sometimes I track back a little to see which way he wants to take us, though.

Akil keeps us stuck to surface streets. Falls Road all the way down to Greenmount, where it dead-ends into a cemetery. That's where we go right. We're on some street for two blocks before jagging left onto Colvin. The Carmelo Anthony Youth Center's on that street. He's a basketball player. Used to play for the Denver Nuggets before he left for somewhere bigger. I guess he grew up here, though, and this red brick building with pictures of little kids lit up by some streetlamps is him giving back. We leave that behind us.

Around, and through, the wind whipping by my ears, the city throws out some night sounds. Bass grumbles of packing trucks idling near stores or at lights. Music in pockets, mostly through car windows. Motown. Radio commercials. Techno. We're on Fayette only for a few seconds but a ways off I hear a woman's scream and I'm not sure if it's the good or bad kind. We're not even on it for a full block before slipping south, almost to the water, before we hit Aliceanna Street and cut back toward the Harbor.

There's a traffic circle, or whatever you call it, in the middle of the road where Aliceanna meets two prongs of South President Street. The circle doesn't have a curb or anything, and

Akil pulls right up into the grass and stops, so I do the same. There's a statue in the middle. It looks like gold flames raising up into the night. We idle by that.

I don't like this, though. Already I don't like it. I tell Akil that and he just nods at me. We don't need to have a conversation about it. He knows this part of the city is too built-up with new stuff, too white. The kind cops must love running people out of. Akil and I have already heard stories about the cops chasing people until they fall off their bikes. It's never happened to us, but there's no saying it can't.

Feels like we've invaded. Like we're holding ground that isn't ours. A white guy in a Mercedes drives around the whole circle slow, mean-mugging us the whole way.

He's waving a phone at me. It must be ringing. Someone must pick up on the other end because he switches his attention to the phone and starts talking fast. It's the cops he called, for sure. Black and gray kids on bikes, well, that means you gotta call 911 or something.

Supposedly, cops can't chase. It's state law. Puts too many innocent Maryland people at risk, supposedly. I say *supposedly* so much because I've heard more stories than you can count about kids getting bumpered up—that's when a police car accidentally on purpose brushes you with its front or back bumper and you take a mad spill. Kids don't get up quick from those either. Bruises, scrapes, busted legs. All that. And I guess—

Far off, I hear a siren and I start because at first I think it's for us, but it's going away—not coming to. I fight my nerves down.

I beat back the urge to just jet out of here. I know Akil wouldn't have brought me here without a dang good reason, but still. This is the kind of waiting that'll give somebody a heart attack.

Akil checks his watch and that's weird for me, because normally he doesn't wear one. See, when you ride a lot and you're accelerating or you're reaching for the brakes, there's a lot of up-and-down on the wrist. Wearing a watch is amateur hour for that reason. At best, it'll pull the hair right out of your arm. At worst, it'll scratch you up worse than an alley cat.

He looks up at the sky then, Akil does, and I'm thinking, *What is this fool doing?*

Because I know we didn't ride down into Copville to stare at the stars.

Akil checks his watch again, and it must be at the time he wants, because he takes it off and zips it into his coat pocket.

"Be looking up," he says.

"For what?"

"When you see it," he says it real serious, "you'll know."

I look up. Around us are some tall buildings, mostly made of glass and lit up from the inside. Sometimes I wonder how much money these companies spend keeping themselves lit up at night. Directly across from me is the brightest one, Legg Mason. It looks like a bunch of lit-up vertical rectangles pushed together in a tower. I turn my eyes back to the street. At this point, I'm sure somebody's called the cops on us and I'm itchy. I don't like sitting around waiting for things to happen. Not out in the open like this.

So since I'm nervous, I talk. I ask something I've been meaning to ask for a while. "Why'd they give you the backpack back anyway? You never said."

I was trying to get my head around what would make Parrot give over something he took.

"You right." Akil looks away, but the tone of voice tells me he's got one of those smiles on again, at least a half of one. "I didn't."

"Fine then," I say. I know when Akil puts his mind to something, that's it. He's not changing it.

"Ayight, since you want to know so bad, I told them I'd trade them a backpack for a ride on my bike."

"No, you didn't."

"Course I did. What'd you think, I just jumped them up like they jumped you?"

I'm about to have a comeback for that, I'm about to ask if he actually followed through on that deal of letting Parrot ride, but right then I hear this loud *fwoop* sound above us, out of nowhere, and I duck and look up to see a parachute floating down and away.

"Ha," Akil says as he revs his engine. "Told you! There he is."

I'm thinking, *There* who *is*? Because there's nobody I know that's crazy enough to jump off a building for no good reason.

"Shit, though," Akil says, and he's got some fear in his voice. "Does it look like he's gonna land all right?"

The wind's carrying the parachute away from us, up South President Street and there's not much traffic, a car here and there, but it's enough to kill anybody that manages to land it.

15

US NOW TOO

That's when we blaze. I'm facing up South President, trying to figure on if I should take the street's right prong full of tail-lights or the left prong full of headlights, when Akil's engine screams and he zips past me, taking the left. That makes it easy for me.

Eas*ier*, anyway.

Akil has to deal with the traffic coming straight at us, and he does it by throwing out wheelies, going up on one wheel, bringing it down, and doing it again—making himself big like they always tell you to do if you see a bear in Colorado. Make yourself bigger. Put your arms up. That's basically what Akil's doing now, except the cars are predators. Especially at thirty-five or forty miles an hour.

It's crazy is what it is.

It's also the most amazing thing I've ever seen. Especially because it works.

Traffic slows, veers off to the side, or stops.

That's when I go too. My heart's in my stomach as I hear cars swerve around him, brakes complaining on their pads, rubber squealing, but I can't look. I'm too busy playing cowboy and taking up both lanes, herding cars off to the right, making them slow down.

At one of the cross-streets, a big black van with one of those flat fronts tries to pull out fast and almost hits me. It honks, long and hard, but I'm already gone, and it's lost behind the cars following me.

All this time I'm looking up whenever I can, head on a swivel, doing my best to track the figure as he's coming down in his parachute—maybe sixty feet above us?—and I know Akil's doing the same and looking up too because I see him out of my peripheral, not so far ahead. Right next to me, a car swerves off my right and goes up over the curb and into a parking sign, knocking it to the sidewalk with a loud *clang*. Shit. You know that's not good.

Can't think about it now, though. Have to keep going.

Above me, the parachuter's getting close. So close that I decide to do something stupid in traffic. I look left and right quick behind me. I got a little bit of a cushion between me and two cars. They're wary, looking at me, so I give them reason to be.

I slam on my brakes until I'm dead stopped and then I

spin my bike underneath me. I'm braking and gassing it at the same time, shifting my weight to my right leg, and laying down a fat line of rubber in a circle all around me—straight 360 degrees.

This stops all traffic on my side.

And I don't know if Akil saw me doing it and does it, or if he had the same idea too, at the same moment, because he knows if he doesn't get these cars stopped, the parachuter's dead.

And it's into this empty asphalt space on my side that the flying dude lands—well, not so much lands as gets both feet on the ground, then tries to run but he's going too fast so his momentum just tumbles him over, ass over head, as he flips a few times and comes to a smack on the pavement with his chute on top of him like a giant collapsed tent.

Right then I think, *Shit, that's it for him.* Dude hit *hard.*

Akil must think the same because he doesn't even cross the divider. He just sits there staring. Not even doing donuts anymore. Just watching. Waiting.

And that's when the silk starts moving, punching up in places, and I know someone's trying to get free. I roll up right close to it, kickstand my bike, and rip the chute back in big handfuls until a person pops up, and I see a face I've only ever seen in videos—and seeing it so familiar, right in front of me, here, after just having jumped off a goddamn building? It sends a shiver up my spine.

It's Kurtis.

No helmet. Shaved head. Headband like basketball players

wear. A low brow and brown eyes set back a little. Skin shining black copper in the glare of headlights. Nose mashed down like he's landed on it a few times.

Holy shit, I think. *It's fucking Kurtis!*

He's mumbling something. I think it's *thank you*, and I don't know how I keep it together. Maybe it's all the headlights on us, all the people staring, and Akil blasting over the divider and shouting, "We got to get the *hell* out of here!"

"Help me get him out of this," I say, and I'm grabbing at the buckles and straps of his harness, trying to figure out how to pry him out when Akil pops the blade on a knife and just saws three damn straps off.

"Done," he says and smiles. "Now, let's gee-oh!"

Even I know that means *go*. For good reason too.

Sirens are coming. Lots of them. Sirens on top of sirens. And I don't know where from. The noise just bounces off buildings every which way and makes it hard to pinpoint the direction.

I hop to my bike. It's still running hot.

Kurtis is still standing there in the middle of the street, looking up at the building he just jumped from, admiring how far he's come and lived, no doubt. He looks shaken, though, like maybe he hit his head. So I yell at him.

"Man, you coming or not?"

He takes a step toward me and stumbles. I throw an arm out and he grabs it.

Akil's behind him, helping him onto the back of my bike. I feel his weight lean forward on me and I know he's locked in.

Of all the people not to be worried about on two wheels, it's this guy. He's the king.

I rip. Straight up South President—away from the traffic jam I created—like a rocket blasting off and leaving the atmosphere. My nervousness burns off around me, it blows away in the wind as I adjust to how different my bike rides with two people on it. It's heavier on the axles. Turns need to be wider.

And the first one comes up faster than I thought.

I'm smart about how I jump the first red light on Lombard. I don't go straight through. That'd be death.

So I slow down enough to get to the little curb ramp, and ride up onto the sidewalk before going a block coming back down to the next little ramp and shooting out into the street again.

Thank god there's no pedestrians.

I go six blocks like this. Twenty. All the while getting insanely lucky because there's no cops anywhere.

They must all be back behind us. Looking for us. Freaking out because some idiot just jumped off a building and into traffic. Either on purpose or by accident. It doesn't even matter.

When we're far enough away from danger, I shout at Kurtis, "Man, I don't know Baltimore. You better tell me where to turn."

So he does. He tells me where to turn. *Left here. No, go straight. Right. Left. Go straight.* One-ways are tough here—Baltimore has too damn many one-way streets—but I'm good with Kurtis guiding me. And Akil follows me for once. I got no idea where I'm going, really. But I know we're out.

I know all those sirens behind me are for Kurtis—well, for us now too. And I feel both excited and terrible about that at the same time.

All that gets worse when some cop lights zip out of a side street, though. The siren blasts almost in my face. Like he was waiting and trying to scare us now, or like he knew which way we were coming from. I don't even know how to say it. One second we were clear, and the next we're not.

I look to Akil to see what to do, but he's smiling at me, like, *I got this.* And then he slows down.

As he drops back I feel it in my stomach like a drop on a roller coaster: he's distracting the cops. He's doing it so we can go free.

Akil always was better at racing than me, and I got a passenger, but still.

I'm in awe as he peels off to my left, waving his arms at the cop, turning around on his seat and putting up two very visible middle fingers before shooting off into the night. Going the opposite way.

When the cop goes with him, I can't really say how big my gratitude is. Lakes. Oceans.

That big.

16

LOST BOYS

Kurtis's house is by Druid Hill Park, really not all that far from me and Akil, just on the other side of the I-85, down 41st, and up Druid Park Drive. I bust a little right on this tiny street called Hilldale because Kurtis said to, and roll up and around to park behind these row homes built on a slant so bad that their roofs don't look like a straight line together, they look like stairs—each house on a lower step than the other.

It's the corner one we park behind. It's the bottommost step in the row of row homes. I ask Kurtis what the address is and he tells me. I pull out my phone Aunt Blue got me only for emergencies and this is one, so I text Akil. Six minutes feels like too many before I hear a bike coming and go poke my head around the corner. I'm about as relieved as anybody can be when I see Akil turn in, no tail behind him. No more cops.

When he gets close, I say, "That was stupid."

"Don't act like you mad," Akil says. "*Somebody* had to take Cogland off you."

I recognize his name. Aunt Blue leaves copies of the *Sun* out when it's pertinent.

That's her word. *Pertinent.* One article was about this kid that died two weeks ago, Evander Brycewell. He was only seventeen. It said this cop—Cogland, his name was—allegedly chased him and Evander panicked and crashed. He bled to death while waiting for an ambulance. This Cogland was under investigation for his role in the death. That's all I remember about that. Newspapers are one thing, but the streets know Cogland.

How he'll beat you if he ever catches you. Broken wrists and ankles. That's what Cogland's about. Getting riders off the street by making sure they can't ride.

I say, "How do you know it was him?"

"The nose, man."

I give him a look, like, *go on.*

"The dude is all forehead." Akil laughs after that, but doesn't say anything else.

I want to know how he got close enough to confirm that in the dark, but I don't ask. Akil's act seems so much more heroic now, taking on the cop with the biggest reputation out there and winning. I don't know how to say a thanks big enough so I leave it, and help Kurtis off my bike instead. He seems a bit more together, especially when he hobbles over to the garage and clicks away at a combination lock before undoing it and lifting the whole door up so we can drag our bikes in. There isn't much room, though.

Because the whole thing is filled with other bikes. There's dirts. Kawasaki Ninjas. Four-wheelers. You name it, Kurtis has got it or probably he had it at one point. There must be ten different kinds in here, all leaning against each other, shoulder to shoulder. Akil and I stop and stare at them until Kurtis says, "Don't be caught looking too long now."

We straighten up when we hear that, get our bikes in there on a lean, and watch as Kurtis locks the door from the inside this time.

"Come on then," he says, sounding like an old man almost.

And I know he's hurt, but this isn't completely the guy I expected from the videos. The guy that mugs and puts his hand in the air. The guy that dances on top of his bike when he's leaning back. Right now, he's not that guy. He's just somebody me and Akil have to help up two steps to get into the house.

"Welcome," he says when we're through the door and it's closed behind us. "This right here is my humble abode."

He clicks a light on and I see we're in a long, rectangular living room that ends in a window and door that must be the front of the row home, looking out onto the park.

And the rest of it doesn't look so humble to me. There's a video game machine like the kind they got in arcades throwing out blue and red squares on the opposite wall from a corner, and what it's lighting up is an old movie poster that has some kid on a BMX bike flying and it just says RAD in some corny letters above his head. My eye went there first, but once I notice it, I realize that you can't see the walls for all the movie posters on them, almost all of them '80s stuff, like Kurtis raided a movie theater that went out of business and found a back room all full of these things that nobody wanted anymore. There's so many they disappear behind the TV, the couch. The only place they aren't is the ceiling or the floor.

It hadn't occurred to me until I saw it, but I wanted it immediately. Something just clicked in me. I wanted this to be what my room looked like if I could do whatever I wanted. Aunt Blue would kill me, though.

Akil's right behind me. Maybe he's thinking the same thing, and he's definitely more entitled to it. He's actually got a house he can do whatever he wants with.

"This is like some Lost Boys business is what this is," I whisper.

"Right," Akil says. "Vampires."

Actually I was thinking *Peter Pan* but I don't disagree with Akil. It's kind of that thing too. Not in exactly that way, but more like it's a little more dangerous here than you'd expect from the decoration.

Being here, I get the feeling I have to be on my game. Can't slip. Can't relax. Can't be looked at as a kid. I know Akil feels the same way. He doesn't need to say it.

Something moves on the couch then, and it takes me a second to realize it's a girl.

She's rubbing her eyes. She's waking up, pushing a blanket off her and stretching her arms up over her head. Just a tank top and little shorts. That's all she has on. You can see a lot of her skin. Almost too much. I look away but I keep her in my peripherals. I can't *not*.

She's round in the right places and skinny in the right places and she's got lips like—I got to leave it at that. She's fine as *hell*, like magazine-cover fine. And that's that.

I see a bookcase kind of wedged into a nook on my left. I decide I should concentrate real hard on that instead, because what does a guy like Kurtis read anyway? There's names in here I've never seen before and can't pronounce. Foreign-looking names. *N-i-e-t-z-s-c-h-e. K-a-f-k-a.* Others like that too. It's real different.

I never would've expected a guy that could ride like a demon to be reading anything, much less stuff nobody can pronounce. But maybe that's just me being stupid, because I ride. And I read too.

Akil doesn't care about these books, though. He's looking at the girl until she notices he's looking, and then he looks at his shoe tops.

"Hello," she says.

"Evening, ma'am," Akil says.

She laughs at that. "I ain't no *ma'am*. *Mademoiselle* maybe. Monika's my name. You can call me Mon."

"Okay," Akil says, "Mon."

"There you go. And who's this with you?"

Akil elbows me. "This's Grey."

"Gray like the color?"

"Yup," Akil says, "but with an *e* in it."

"Cool." She tilts her neck to the side until it pops. "Where's Kurtis at?"

Akil shrugs.

Out front, tires screech and some big kind of vehicle hits the curb, rolls over it, and comes to a thumping stop.

I give Akil a *did-you-hear-that?* look. He quick-nods at me.

But then he does one better. He takes his knife out and holds it by his side. He's being quiet about it, but I still hear the blade flick out.

"Uh," he says without taking his eyes off the front door, "you expecting somebody, Kurtis?"

Kurtis shuffles out of what I could guess is the kitchen and he's got this old-man-looking ice bag on his head. It's one of those rubbery blue things, with polka dots and a circular top you have to screw down so the ice doesn't leak after it melts into water.

"Baby," Mon says as she jumps up, "baby, what'd you *do*?"

Mon's shorts are tight on her backside. Akil's locked right on it, eyes wide. I elbow him back.

And that's when a hard knock hits the door. I don't jump, but I want to.

It doesn't faze Kurtis, though. He's already sitting on the couch, tugging up the leg of his jeans, showing his girl this killer road rash he caught from flipping and skidding on the asphalt. Mon squeals when she sees blood and runs upstairs.

Me and Akil, we both want to look at her as she goes.

We don't, though. We're both too locked on the front door, waiting to see what comes next.

17

SOME KIND OF NATURAL

Holding the ice pack to his head, Kurtis raises himself up, goes over to the door, stands beside it, and undoes the latch. I get why he stood off to the side of it then, because he knew whoever it was would want to bust right in. And they do.

The door slams the nearby wall and puts a doorknob dent in a poster for *Smokey and the Bandit*. Kurtis makes a face at the sound of that, like, *c'mon, man*.

There's three of them standing in the doorway. The one in front's the biggest, looking like a thin Biggie Smalls. He blocks the others out like an eclipse. And he looks crazy angry. His whole face is just a twisted-up mess under his black woolie hat, which matches his black Windbreaker and black shirt and black jeans. They're all dressed like that. The one in front, Thin Biggie, he turns to Kurtis and breathes out all heavy and hard like he's about to set some shit on fire. And then, well, he looks at us.

And he points. At *me*.

When he does it, I feel it in my stomach. And he says, "Are these the motherfuckers?"

He's talking plural, but he's looking only at me.

Through the door behind him, I see a black van with a flat-front nose on it. That's when everything clicks. I've seen that van before. It almost hit me when it tried to pull into traffic. I don't need to be Sherlock Holmes to figure out that this was Kurtis's rescue team and they failed.

We showed them up, disrespected them by being better, and now they're upset. So upset that Biggie repeats what he said earlier, but now he's walking toward us, pounding the floor with his boots, *thump-athumpa* is what their soles sound like as they're passing the couch, and right then is when Akil steps in front of me.

Just like that.

Doesn't think. Doesn't question it. Just sees a six-foot dude walking tough and steps right in front of me.

I'll never forget that. Not as long as I live.

You sure find out who your friends are when somebody wants to punch your face through the back of your head.

But something slows Thin Biggie when he gets close. Akil's blade. Biggie eyes it like he's not sure if it's real at first, but when he brings his eyes back up to Akil's, Akil just nods, like, *yeah, idiot, it's real*. And something crucial happens right then, because Thin Biggie takes a step back, and pulls up the bottom of his shirt to show us a handgun tucked in his waistband.

That's when it's my turn to step back. Akil doesn't move an inch.

"You no-account bitches blocked us out!" Thin Biggie points his finger hard at me again. "And you in particular."

Akil brings his knife up slow and Biggie's hand goes back to where it was at his side. Real quick too. But this time it lands on the hilt.

"We had it," Thin Biggie says. "*Believe* that."

Monika's coming down the stairs with all manner of creams and medicines and Band-Aids when she says, "Had what, Darryl?"

Thin Biggie twitches when she says it. That must be his name. *Darryl.* He says, "We had Kurtis's back, Mon!"

She gets to the bottom step and blinks at him. "Then how come Kurtis came back with these two and not you?"

It's cold logic. Something Aunt Blue would pull. I'm impressed. It's obvious just from seeing this that she holds down the home front with a vengeance.

You can tell he's got no answer for that when, after a second, Darryl only says, "Because."

Mon sweeps by the couch and drops the medicines off next to Kurtis before getting next to Darryl, not in his face, but close. "What are you even doing with that? You about to put somebody's eye out?"

He stares at her for a second. "Maybe."

"*Uh huh*. You know who wasn't about *maybe*? Samurai weren't about maybe. They pull a sword and it's getting done. You can't ever be that guy that's about maybe. Not in this city. And I'm not trying to jump on you here, but look at this with me right quick." She nods at Akil, at the knife still in his hand. "See those eyes? He's not about maybe. He's got nothing to lose. He would've cut you if he knew what you were to Kurtis. But since he didn't, he didn't."

Mon turns a gaze to Akil and nods. Darryl blinks. Me and Akil blink back, but we're just kind of watching Mon in awe now. At how calm she is. At how she broke Akil down so quick, and how true it seems with his mom gone, he really does have nothing to lose. It's crazy how Mon just projects this ability to handle whatever and the room seems to respond to it. That's when she takes a step forward and her voice goes down like it's just for Darryl then, even though we all can hear it.

"Takes all kinds to make a team." She hits a good pause then before finishing out with, "You know who told me that once? *You* did. When you first wanted to join up. And I might just be guessing, but I'm pretty sure that's what they want too."

She means me and Akil. Watching her talk, and seeing Darryl nod, I see they got the same noses. It all makes sense to me then. They must be brother and sister. That's why she's breaking him down and he's letting her. She's smart too, though. She knows just how far to break him. Too much and he'll blow up or keep it all inside and do something stupid later. Just enough and maybe he'll learn. It's some Aunt Blue mind-trick stuff she'd use on me. I know it. This Mon, she's worth learning from.

Darryl drops his shirt, covering the gun, and Akil puts his knife away. Fair's fair. "There we go," Mon says, and moves back to the couch to sit next to Kurtis.

"This crew needs way more females, that's all I'm saying. I can't put up with this caveman shit all the time. Y'all need to be recruiting girls that can ride. Straight up."

Darryl looks to Kurtis and something I can't speak to passes between them and Kurtis shrugs.

"They saved me, man. You didn't. Facts is facts." Kurtis talks at Darryl in a calm way, slow, all cool about it, like everything he says is the ultimate truth, and all the time he's talking, Mon rolls his jean legs up and gets to work on his cuts.

Darryl makes a noise like he's kissing his teeth.

"Well, we did *something* for you," he says. "We scooped that parachute up so the police couldn't get it."

"And I *appreciate* that." Kurtis winces when Mon brings out peroxide and dabs him with a cotton ball weighed down with it, but his voice doesn't change. "I do."

Darryl sniffs before breaking eye contact with Kurtis and turns his attention back on me and Akil. "You two still fucked the whole plan up. Stopping traffic like that? That was stupid."

I don't know where the words come from. I didn't even know they were inside me until they're already on my tongue and I'm saying, "Maybe you should've had a better plan."

That does it. Darryl starts nodding at that, almost like he's agreeing with bad thoughts he's got deep inside, and his eyes are everywhere else but back on me. He slings a look at the guys behind him, and then to the ceiling before saying, "Man, I know this milky-tea-looking piece of shit didn't just say that to me."

Of course, he's talking about me. How I'm not black enough. How I'm grey. I guess this is him trying to salvage something from the situation, and I get it, but I still feel a tingle at the bottom of my throat then, like a spider running over my collarbones, and I don't know how I feel about those words he just said. It's kind of a jumble. It's kind of mad and weird and wounded, mostly.

Kurtis smirks. "He's right, though. You know that, right? Pride aside, we should've had a better plan. And after how he just rode, you're gonna go at him like that? That's not just cold. What's your name anyway, little man?"

"Grey," I say.

"How long you've been riding them bikes?"

"BMX bikes almost my whole life." I say that before adding, "but dirt bikes for about two months. Give or take."

The whole room goes quiet.

"Two months?" Kurtis laughs at that. "Two fucking months? Are you kidding me with that?"

Akil pops off then. "It's the straight truth. He's some kind of natural, this one."

Darryl's still mad at me, don't get me wrong, he still looks like he wants to put my lights out, but even he's blinking at that and chewing his lip.

And the room has changed around him. Some heat got let out of it somehow.

Maybe it's the laughter that did it, I don't know. It definitely played a role.

But some things you just can't explain, and definitely not in the moment. Like how close to Akil I'm feeling right now. Just like Jamar. Like brothers.

And I don't think I could ever say to him how proud I am that we just did some soldiering side by side. How we rode the streets like they were ours.

And already I get to thinking on how danger glues people together, makes them one team. United against everybody else.

Or how there's never been a better feeling for me in this world than knowing someone has my back.

Not ever.

18

FIRING SQUAD

Back at Akil's, when the bikes are both up, when we're in Akil's room and we've been watching Kurtis's videos all over again, we can't stop talking about everything that happened. We tell stories. We replay how it went down step by step with our mouths. Adding details. Adding things we remember. That gets us excited all over again. We do sound effects. When we first left that traffic circle, it was like *brrrrrrnnt*. Doing 360 circles to back off a bunch of cars, it was like *da-dran-da-da-da*. Both those are mine.

But then Akil says, "No. It was like—"

I say, "Oh, it was like what?"

But I'm not hurt he disagrees or anything. We're just funning.

"It was like"—Akil makes this face like maybe he got smacked and he's not sure how many teeth he has left before he starts spitting almost—"*bram-bram-brammmmm*. That's the real sound of the brake and gas going at each other."

"What the hell you talking, *bram bram bram*? Sounding like a little kid trying to say *bran muffin* and not even getting it right."

"*Bram.*" Akil looks all kinds of serious. He even crosses his arms like the conversation's been decided and he won. "That's the sound. Right there. Done."

"Your ears are broken," I say. "Mad broken."

"I could say the same to you," he says.

"So say it then!"

When I shout that, it starts us going all over again. I laugh. I laugh till I have trouble breathing. It gets worse when he says my traffic circle breakout noise sounds like *I'm* having trouble saying the word *burnt*. We laugh so much I forget about just about everything except a question I've been needing answered since the moment a dude fell out of the Baltimore city sky dragging a parachute with him.

I nod at a close-up of Kurtis leaning back on a four-wheeler that's freeze-framed in the browser behind Akil.

"Something I got to know," I say, "but how did you know about that jump?"

"I don't even know if I feel like telling you."

"I think you do, though," I say.

He turns away in his spinny chair, facing his body back to the computer, even though he's still eyeing me. He's not saying anything.

"Fine, then. I see how it is. Drag me out in the dead of night to do something I don't even know is about to be the most dangerous thing ever."

He laughs. "Yeah, but you liked it though."

"I *ended up* liking it. But going out in the dark, and being in the dark because you wouldn't tell me, that wasn't cool."

He shakes his head at me like I'm too smart for my own good. He says, "Maybe I'm one of them psychics. You ever think of that?"

"First thing I thought of," I say, "but I guess you knew that, huh?"

Akil looks at me hard like he's trying to come up with a comeback for that but he ends up just smiling.

"It's really not all that special," he says. "A girl I used to kick it with is best friends with Kurtis's girl, Mon. And she told me."

"You ever met Mon before?"

"No."

"So your ex told you? How'd she even know?"

Akil's shaking his head at the designation. "Not my ex, but yeah. Mon told her and told her not to tell anybody, but the girl—not my ex, but the one I used to kick it with—told me because she wants to maybe get back together with me or something."

It's funny how sometimes things are so much simpler than you think they are. I had it all built up in my head that Akil hacked an email or he met Kurtis somehow and this was all just some kind of initiation that no one in Kurtis's crew got told about, but—

Something hits me then. Something I forgot about. Panic punches me in the belly.

My aunt. The time she's getting home. "Oh shit," I say. "What time is it?"

Akil leans his face real close to the clock on his computer.

"Seven seventeen." He leans back then, not even knowing what he's saying at the moment he saying it. "Hey, wasn't your aunt supposed to get off at seven?"

I'm up on my feet and down the stairs in a hurry.

Akil's right behind me.

We don't even need to talk. We push his bike out the front and get the door locked up behind us and then we rip.

Akil goes almost eighty up 41st. It still takes too long.

On my aunt's street, we actually stop a block and a half away, get off the bike, and walk it in so it won't be loud.

But it's too late though. Dawn's already peeking out all over. It's stringing itself through the tops of trees like a bunch of light-colored ribbons you can see through.

Every house on the block has no lights on because people inside are still asleep.

My aunt, she just worked a long shift. The living room light's on, though. I see the silhouette shape of her head and shoulders through the front window. She's sitting there. Waiting for me.

And that's an uh-oh. An uh-oh like you'd never believe.

Because Aunt Blue's old school. Still, maybe my only saving grace is I didn't break one of her rules, even if I broke an implied one, and I know how she's gonna be so disappointed in me that she even has to tell me I can't stay out all night. And definitely not in this city. *B-more eats black folks.* She said that to me once when we were on the airplane coming out. I guess she thought I could handle it on account of my momma.

It's a hungry city, she said. *It puts them in their graves early and on time.*

I know Rule Five, going to therapy, will probably be coming back with a vengeance, though. Because I've been doing so good in school—doing so *well* in school—she's been letting me slide on setting up appointments. I don't see that happening anymore. No way. No how.

Right now I'm remembering the look Aunt Blue gave me when she reserved the right to add new rules when necessary. How hard it was. I know that's the kind of firing squad I'm walking into.

Akil doesn't know what to say, so I start it.

"I don't know how this's about to end up," I say to him. "But thanks." I put my hands up and exhale. "For tonight, and just for everything."

"Good luck in there, man. You know if she throws you out, though, you always got a place to stay."

I nod at that, real grateful, and then I turn and walk up the walkway.

I don't hear Akil take off right away. I know he's watching me. I know he feels bad. Like it's his fault. This'll cut him deeper than he'll ever say. Because he already lost his momma, and he didn't get an Aunt Blue in return.

And nobody knows how lucky I am to have her more than Akil Williams.

My stomach's acting like a blender inside me. One stuck on the highest setting too. I don't think my aunt'll throw me out. Not after all this with my momma, the move, a new school. But I can't honestly say for sure.

She might send me away, though.

If not Chicago or Texas, because they don't have any kind of room for me, then probably boarding school.

She's not above that, I think. *No, sir, she's sure not.*

I take a breath before I take my key out, unlock the door, and walk in.

19

FOUR LITTLE WORDS

The living room only has one light on, the reading lamp by the big brown chair. Aunt Blue's sitting in it, not looking at me. She's got her face in a book. Her reading glasses are yellow in that light and the forehead shadow that drops down over her eyes makes her look like a statue. She's doing this on purpose. It's her showing me I'm not important right now.

I know how Momma would be in this situation: She'd fly at me and slap me and it'd be like a bird attack—fast and scary and squawky but if you'd just cover up it'd be over quick. That was Momma. Her anger burned hot but fast and then we'd be friends again. Well, not friends, but mother and son and I'd be close to forgiven. After that, she'd apologize and I'd apologize, and we'd work out a new plan for how not to do whatever-it-was-I-did again. That was that.

But this? This is a new kind of thing.

I hear Aunt Blue sigh deep and turn the page of her book. After that, it's the type of quiet where you're afraid to move. For a second, I think maybe if I hold my breath and walk up the stairs everything will be fine. It'd be my free pass. But I'm not that stupid. Aunt Blue never let a mosquito get away with flying, and she sure as heck's not going to let me free.

"Aunt Blue, I'm sor—"

Her finger interrupts me. It's her right index and she sticks it in the air like a teacher. She doesn't even look up to do it, just keeps her eyes on the page as she holds it in the air, like, *you better give me one moment and then it's your turn.*

I make a conscious decision not to play any Momma cards right then, because that wouldn't be fair. Besides, Aunt Blue will already be thinking it. The fact my momma is dead will already be the reason I'm out so late, the reason why I'm so lost, and that hurts more. Because it isn't the reason. There's a reason beyond that reason.

After three more long pages, Aunt Blue closes the book, puts it on the end table with its crocheted doily on it that Grand-momma made, takes her glasses off, and just straight *stares* at me. She puts her eyes on my eyes and I just want to confess it's so bad. Because just with a look she makes it clear how sad and mad and disappointed I made her. How it's my fault. It's one of those looks. It reaches down into my soul and makes me sorrier than I ever was for worrying her.

When I can't take it anymore, I look at my shoes and try

again. "I'm sorry, Aunt Blue. Real sorry. I shouldn't've been out so late."

"You shouldn't have been out *at all*." Aunt Blue's got that useful kind of mad voice that makes you want to confess everything. "Where you been at?"

Four words, that's it. *Where. You. Been. At.*

Aunt Blue knows how to talk proper. Big-time, she does. But now I can tell she's crazy mad at me, the ghetto comes out of her like a dam breaking. Like she keeps it hidden inside until she can't hold it anymore. And it's broken now. And she wants me to know I broke it. I brought the ghetto out of her. And the way it's about to jump into her words, her sentences, tells me I'm in deeper trouble than I thought. Lets me know she knows about these streets and I can't tell her anything about them, but she sure can tell me. She's seen it. Lived it. Every day she goes to work she still treats the ills of it.

Nobody understands the sadness of Baltimore like Aunt Blue. Nobody tries to fight it away from her door harder. And here I am, walking in with it all over me. She can smell it. She knows I've been up to no good.

And she's up now. Her hands are on her hips. Her neck's even moving when she says, "I *said*, where you been at?"

There's no way to win against that voice. I know I did wrong, so I decide to tell her the truth. And once I get going, it all spills out of me in a rush. About Parrot and them, but I leave out the part where I stole the pipe and hit somebody with it. But I talk about Akil, how he lost his momma too and how that made us brothers and he's my only friend and we ride together. We get on his bikes and we just—

"Those bikers ain't nothing but drug dealers. Jackers. Every time I hear that sound, I know they're just about to rip somebody off and get out quick."

"That's not true, Aunt Blue. There's some like that, but not us. Most are just kids wanting to ride. To be in control for once. To escape."

Until that's out of my mouth, I didn't even really know I felt that way. But that's what it is to me. A time to be in control. An escape. A vacation from the feelings and thoughts about my momma's death, and being separated from my brother and sisters, about having to move to a new city I've never even been to before. About *everything*.

She says, "Escape from what?"

And she says it almost like I'm talking about her and this nice home she works for, like I want to escape from this floor holding us up right now, this roof over our heads, this heat clicking on and coming through the vents above us right then.

I say, "You know from what."

And I don't mean it to come out harsh, but I can't say it any other way.

Aunt Blue keeps that hard look on me, that you're-an-ice-cube-and-I'm-about-to-melt-you look. But there's something else in it now. A little thing. And it's her thinking, trying to figure how truthful I'm being. She's eyeing me to make sure this isn't to do with her. But she knows it isn't. She knows it's to do with my momma. And this is how I run from it. But it's something more too. Something bigger.

So I kind of change it up a bit. Not placing blame, really, but trying to show her how I got here.

"Aunt Blue, I don't mean to be rude or disrespectful but you started this," I say, and when she reels back like she's about to fight me, I keep going with, "and not like in a bad way! But you got me reading. You got me thinking about art and what it means to me. How to express my truth."

"Art is not motorbikes, Grey Monroe. Not a damn thing about riding them is your truth. My lord! What is *wrong* with you?" She throws her hands up in the air, almost like she can't handle me alone. Like she needs a little help from above. When they come back down, she sighs hard.

"The problem with saying things," Aunt Blue finally says, "is you never know how somebody's going to take it. You try and try but . . ."

She smirks like those words are for me and not for me at the same time.

"Feel alive for a little bit, be dead for a long time." Aunt Blue shakes her head at me like I should know better having been through what I've been through. "You have any idea how many motorcycle accident victims I see a week?"

I shake my head.

"More than's worth counting," she says. "And the worst ones are the ones that the doctor tells them they can't ride anymore and they nod and then three months later I see them back with a severed spinal cord and they're crying all about how they shouldn't have done it and now they're paralyzed and you know what I think?" She leans closer to me. "I think, you did it to yourself. Ain't nobody to blame but *you*."

In her eyes, I can almost see her fears for me. Me in a mess on the road. Me bleeding. Me not doing the things I'm supposed to be doing. Graduating. Going to college. Getting out if I want to.

"Is that what you want? To be paralyzed? To be *dead*?"

She's not even talking to me. She's talking to the air around me. Moving her eyes to it. Above my head. Above my shoulder. To the cutout space between my body and my arm while it hangs loose at my side.

I stare at the soles of her shoes. From where I'm standing, I can only see the tips of them, but I'm hoping they'll move. She stays so still though. And that just twists me up inside. So much I feel like all I need at that minute is just to see her soles move. Even a little. Just—something.

And that's when I say something stupid.

"Aunt DeeDee," I say. *DeeDee* is short for *Deidre*. That's Aunt Blue's real given name. "Why're you called Blue anyway?"

That does it. The feet shift.

They jerk back like I hit her somehow and they need to rebalance her weight.

But I can breathe again, and for a second that feels so good, but only for a second. Because it stops feeling good right when I see that her soles shift too much.

They're turning now, taking steps. And that's how Aunt
Blue walks away. Not that she goes far. She just goes straight
into her bedroom and shuts the door and locks it.

A door getting locked when you're trying to talk to someone
is about the worst sound on earth. It's a stoplight you can't blow
through or take the sidewalk to get around. But I can take it.
It's a morbid thought, but I think, *At least she's not dead.* I think,
We can talk later.

Still, I stand there for a long time hoping the door will open
and when it doesn't, I turn off the reading lamp and go upstairs
to bed.

20

WEIRD PEACE

In the morning is Part Two. Only good thing about going out late on a Friday is you can come home and sleep a little and wake up late and it's still morning—barely.

I didn't sleep much. I was in and out of it mostly. Thirty minutes here, forty there, and I was still tired as hell when the clock told me it was about noon and I heard Aunt Blue moving around in the kitchen downstairs, the soles of slippers going *skish-skish* back and forth while she made food.

That sound made me feel good, knowing she was down there, but it also made me feel bad at the same time. Bad like I didn't do enough or say enough last night. Like I should've done better.

So I go downstairs and stand in the doorway at first, just watching. Not sure if I'm allowed to come in. Aunt Blue knows

I'm here. She's just making me hang out in our silence. It's part of the punishment, I think. She's set up at the kitchen table, wearing her purple bathrobe with the fuzzy collar and cuffs she rolls back up to the elbows so they look like fuzzy donuts on her arms. She's got two pieces of toast in front of her and both are black on the crust and brown in the middle how she likes them.

Next to her plate is an open jar of mustard, a little of that red Old Bay seasoning people around here like so much, a closed jar of mayo, a slice of cheese still in its wrapper, and a little black box of turkey slices with its clear cover pulled back. It's a sandwich but she hasn't made it all the way yet. Right now it's just a bunch of different pieces yet to be something more.

"This Akil," she says to me after a bit of us pretending like neither one is in the room, "what's he like?"

I tell her he's quiet. I tell her he's a good dude, just lonely. I tell her he doesn't trust people easy. I tell her his momma died, but this time I tell her how.

"And where's he living?"

I tell her about the house on 41st and Falls Road. Right by the bus stop.

She nods at that like she's a detective and that was a crucial chunk of information she was missing. After that, we get down to the important stuff. She nods at the chair across from her and I know well enough to walk over there and sit down in it.

She wants me to stop riding. She's real clear about it.

But when I tell her I don't know how I can do that, she just stares at the turkey.

She says she's serious. I say that I am too. And we go back and forth a little. It's like tug-of-war but with words.

But she lets go of the rope after a few minutes of that, drops the subject, and it throws me off.

She doesn't push as hard on not riding as I expect her to. If this is coming from anywhere, I think it's because she knows I've been missing BMX, and missing Jamar. She'd never want me to think she has compassion, but she does.

And seeing that makes me want to reach out and hug her, but I know I can't yet. We're not done. So I tell her I've been thinking about it and I'll go see a psychologist for her. Rule Six of hers.

"I need to do that for you," I say.

"For *you*," she says. "You'll see one for you. Because it's good for your mental health and it's what you should do, not because you *think* it gets you out of me being mad—because it'll help you."

I pick up the empty pepper shaker shaped like a raven (the salt one's a dove) and look at it. Not because it interests me, but because I don't know what to do with my hands and her eyes are so big how they take me in, trying to show me how she sees me.

"I'm not trying to be rude or anything, Aunt Blue, but can I just ask why that's even a rule?"

"Because I had to do it once and it helped me."

That hangs around in the air for a bit between us. I get the feeling whatever that thing is, whatever it was, made her get named Aunt Blue. She gets to scraping her toast with mustard then and for the first time today, she looks into my eyes and I look back into hers, into the blacks of them—the pupils.

I imagine for a second that I'm reaching down inside her, invisibly, and I'm convincing her that this is the only thing I've got that keeps me growing and moving forward.

This's the time I decide to tell her my secret. To show her I trust her. To seal the deal somehow.

"I saw him, Aunt Blue."

She says, "Saw who?"

"I saw my dad with blood on him. Momma's blood. On that day when, you know."

These words coming out, they're like weights I didn't even know I was carrying until I dropped them. I've never told her any of this before. I've never told anybody.

Jamar knows because he knows. He saw it too.

She stops scraping her cold toast and puts it down. The knife too.

Aunt Blue makes a face at me like she's going to cry right then and there. She says, "The twins saw too?"

"No," I say. "I pushed them behind me."

"That's good," she says. "You did right."

After that, she puts her sandwich together. The mustard on the right toast, the mayo on the left. Dash of Old Bay on the mayo. I've never seen her do that before.

"That's some bayo right there," she says like she's reading my mind. "That's my special trick."

She unwraps the cheese and places it on the mustard. She

takes two slices of turkey and drapes them over the bayo. When her sandwich is made, it's like we've reached this weird peace. And I know we're there because she says, "I've got conditions."

The first is I better not even be thinking about dropping out of school, because if I did that, she'd kill me herself and bury me in the backyard. I know killing and dying's nothing to joke about, but she sure doesn't look like she's funning when she tells me that.

So, that's that. Keep going to school, keeping doing good in it. Well. Doing well. My grades can't slip. If even one does—like from an A to an A minus—I'm grounded until forever. No bikes. No rides. No Akil. Nothing but books.

"That's fair," I say to that.

"I don't care nothing about fair," she says. "You're a minor."

After that, she drops another condition on me: I can't go out at night anymore. If I go out even once at night without telling her, I'm done. I need to follow the traffic laws. Never bait police like some of the other boys do. I also need to license my bike through the state, get a little plate on it. Do it legal.

I tell her I don't own one. I just borrow Akil's old bike.

"We'll see what we can do about that," she says.

I don't know what that means really, but I kind of file that information away to ask about another time, because she's already moving on, telling me how she wants me to ride with a helmet.

"If you don't protect that brain of yours, you can't do it," she says. "End of."

"Okay." I say it even though I'm already cringing thinking about how stupid I'll look. "But only one that covers my head, not my face."

"Why not your face?" Aunt Blue folds her arms at me. "I'm talking like a full helmet with that chin bar or whatever-they-call-it and a visor that slides down."

"I can't, Aunt Blue."

"Why can't you?"

"Because I'm no invisible man," I say. "I need to be seen. I've got to."

Her folded arms get tighter when I say that, like she's hugging herself almost, or protecting herself against something.

I think she knows if she tried to put me in boarding school, I'd run away. If she threw me out, I'd go to Akil's. She wants me close enough to keep an eye on, close enough to influence, close enough to make me come out good.

And still I see fear in her eyes, and I don't want her to feel that, but I can't help it, you know?

This is my thing. Riding is in me. It *is* me.

21

SAFETY CITY

In north Druid Park there's this little model town called Safety City. Actually, it's not so little. It's taller than people and maybe about the width and length of four tennis courts squashed all together. But the cool thing is that it has buildings and streets with painted-out road lines and stop signs above left-turn-only signs and working streetlights five feet off the ground. That last part got me. Actual working streetlights in the middle of a park. It's got street names too: Helen Krolus Way, Dickerson Street, Reading Road. It's even got a little conference pavilion in it that you can't even get in unless you go on your hands and knees and then sit down in it. The whole thing's crazy, but in a good way. It's less like a city got shrunk down than it is like a miniature model train town got blown up to adult size. And to us, it's a place to trick it up and get nice.

I brought my BMX here. First time I've been on that thing in forever. Felt good taking it off the plastic wrap, and it was fun riding out with it, going down 41st and holding the edge of the right handle bar in my left hand, watching the tires spin as it went the speed limit with me. It was like my sidecar almost. I imagined it had an invisible rider on it.

"This here's to teach kids safety," Akil says as he eyes Safety City, clears his throat, and spits on the parking lot we're all standing in. "I never got brought here as an elementary school kid, though. I think it's for white kids."

It's early in the morning, and I mean *early*—so dang early no one's around. It's only just gone dawn and me, Akil, Kurtis, and Kurtis's cousin, Little Nate, are all here staring at this grown-up doll town and wondering how we're gonna do something unsafe in it.

Word is they call Nate little on account of how big he is, two hundred pounds if he's an ounce, and all of that at five foot six. He's got a camera slung around his neck and Kurtis says his face looks like a bowling ball, with the finger holes being his eyes and mouth.

I don't know that that's fair exactly. I think it's just cousins funning, but I can see Nate doesn't like that description too much and Kurtis knows that Nate doesn't like it so he uses it more. Personally, I only just met Nate, but I like him. He's quiet and he's funny. He does voices and stuff. He's at the art school here, at the Maryland Institute College of Art, the same one the documentary dude went to.

I've seen his movie about dirt bikers from around here. We've all seen it, but Kurtis schooled me on what it meant to him yesterday.

"Not everybody's a twelve o'clock boy, you know. Just because you ride around Baltimore don't make you one. They're a pack, and like, I'm cool with them. I'm cool with Wheelie Wayne and Superman, and they're cool with me, but we're different kinds of animals."

Kurtis backtracks a little, saying how he really dug the movie, it just isn't him is all. "Because I'm more than just riding bikes. I push *limits*."

The way he says that, *I push limits*, sticks to me. It kind of hits me in the ears and rides down to my chest where it lands and gets my heart going. Kurtis says the word *limits* like they're things to be eyed and sized up and destroyed. Something to drop a bomb on.

And I like that. I like it a lot. But I'm curious what he means about the animals. I say, "What do you mean about being different animals?"

"I'm no pack animal," Kurtis says. "That's what I mean. I'm not a wolf."

Little Nate jumps on this because I think he senses a joke coming. "So what animal are you then?"

Kurtis is busy staring at the lock on the chain strung through the fence gate. "I haven't thought it out yet."

"Well, maybe you should. I mean, are you like a panther?"

Little Nate says, and I can tell he's leading up to something. "Or a pig? You know, *pigs* aren't pack animals. Maybe you're that."

Kurtis gives him an almighty death stare and then turns his attention back to the matter at hand: getting through the chain. He puts a crowbar he brought through the chain and tries to lever it. Once, twice. Nothing. He shifts his feet and tries from another angle.

"Big cats are cool," he finally says.

"But big cats have packs, or prides or whatever, and you do kind of have a pack. If you don't, what are we?"

Man, Little Nate just loves to needle. Picking at Kurtis is practically his favorite thing to do. He reminds me a lot of Jamar. In a good way, though.

Kurtis shoves the chain once more. It rattles and strains but doesn't give. "You ain't my pack, that's for damn sure." Kurtis tries again, this time kind of spinning the bar as if it were an old-time airplane propeller, the kind you had to push to start that I saw because we're studying flight in my applied science and engineering class. He turns the chain against itself and I hear it groan a little before it rolls and gives, dropping to the fence in two different pieces.

Kurtis has a real big smile on his face, showing the whitest of white teeth when he says, "You're all here on your own recognizance."

He pulls the chain through by the lock like he's pulling a

snake out of a tree by its neck and slaps it to the ground with a jingly *whack*.

"Wow," Little Nate says, and looks at me with wide eyes and then at Akil, and for a second I think he's gonna talk about how Kurtis pulled the chain off but then he says, "that's a big-ass word. *Recognizance*."

"Yeah," Akil says, joining in, "a word like that you only learn in the system." He means jail. Juvenile hall. Either. Or both. I'm not really sure.

And I'm aware how they can do this together. Baltimore kids chipping at each other. Taking digs. But there's this invisible wall that stops me from doing it too.

There's still too much Colorado in me and they know it. If I tried to chime in, they'd turn on me. Even Akil. Just to show me where my place was, on the outside, but just a little. Till I know better. Till I understand the ropes and the inside jokes. Till I can tell Sandtown from Cherry Hill. Till I know Baltimore through and through, basically.

"Man, whatever," Kurtis says. "We doing this or not?"

Little Nate's got his camera out and he's filming the big white sign out in front of the place. WELCOME, it says in cursive, and then under it are the words, BALTIMORE'S MODEL SAFETY CITY. Next to the lettering is a blue map of Maryland with a yellow stoplight stuck over the left side of it. Little Nate pans from that to the front gate, where a NO TRESPASSING sign about the size of my head says, VIOLATORS WILL BE

PROSECUTED TO THE FULLEST EXTENT OF THE LAW.

I gulp at that because I already know how Aunt Blue feels about it, and I say a little apology to her in my head as I take my helmet off, because there's just no way I'm wearing it in here. On the streets, maybe. But not doing stunts.

22

TEN SIZES BIGGER

Hell yes, this's illegal. It's obviously trespassing and probably breaking and entering and maybe three other things that I don't even know too. A few days ago, Aunt Blue said how I couldn't do anything illegal and I didn't exactly say yes, but I didn't say no, and I definitely kind of led her to believe I wouldn't, so now, staring at Safety City, I know I'm about to cross a line, and the worst part is, I want to.

I knew this would happen if I kept hanging with Kurtis. I mean, the dude jumps off buildings. (I kind of left that part out when I told Aunt Blue the truth.)

"The thing about being an outlaw," Kurtis says to Little Nate's camera right then, "is you got to operate *outside* the law. Otherwise, you aren't that. Simple."

This outlaw comes prepared too. He pulls an extra chain

out of his backpack. It's almost the exact length of the one he just busted with the crowbar. He lays this new one out on the ground at the foot of the fence. The metal rings as it strings out.

Kurtis explains now how the plan was always to kung fu their chain in half but leave their lock. After that, we leave the new length of chain so they don't have to replace the old one themselves. So nobody loses. No property is damaged without being replaced. In fact, all they have to do is use the key to unlock the lock and put it on the new chain they string around the front gate in order to get locked back up again.

I follow Kurtis and Akil in. Little Nate comes in walking behind us, keeping the camera up and recording. I only wheel my BMX in beside me and leave Akil's old dirt bike in the parking lot because I'm not totally comfortable with freestyle on it yet. The thing is just too damn heavy to me right now. With its frame and its engine, the weight is totally different to BMXing. I mean, I've seen what Kurtis can do. The way he can guide his bike is just like Mozart must've been on a piano. It does what he wants.

I'm not there yet, though. But I'm still nice on my BMX. Nicer than most anybody knows yet, and I like that. It's my element of surprise.

When we're going in, Akil goes left, Kurtis goes right, and I go up the main road and take it in as I push my BMX beside me.

Being surrounded by buildings only a couple feet taller than you makes me feel like a giant, like Godzilla or something, but not as powerful. I mean, I know I couldn't punch them to pieces, but still, it makes me feel strong, almost like I grew ten sizes bigger and the world stayed the same.

This is how I scan the place: I look for stuff that would launch me. That's it.

Pretty simple, I guess.

Doesn't take me long to find something good either.

Behind this big, red, British phone booth–looking thing is a tiny redbrick building about waist high with a white roof like a pyramid. It's my first target instantly.

Kurtis cruises by me and sees me heading for it on my BMX, so he says, "How high you think you can hit off of that?"

"I don't know," I say. "Maybe five feet. If that."

"So if I ride under and go full back"—Kurtis means if he rides under the tiny streetlights with his body flat and vertical on his bike, toes by the handlebars, head by the back tire—"can you jump over me and make the landing?"

"Maybe," I say, looking from the building to the little road beside it. "I don't know though. Depends on a few things."

Depends on how good my tires do on that roof. Depends on how rusty I am.

Depends on how low Kurtis can get. Like I said, a few things.

But this's how a stunt gets born. Asking questions. Pushing each other. And it already feels sort of natural, this back and forth.

Seeing what's possible by finding that limit and then figuring out a way to say *fuck you* to it. To say, *you can't hold me.* I can do this. And I can do more.

I haven't felt this since me and Jamar did our thing. Sized up walls and obstacles and figured out how we could use them to our benefit.

It makes me too happy, this feeling, like I can't wipe a smile off my face. So I don't. I just let it be as the morning works its way from this purple-greyish thing to orange. Somewhere in the distance I hear seagulls squawking at each other. Maybe they're in the lake down the hill, but I don't know.

"I got to test this out," I say, and first I take a quick lap to feel my BMX under me. I carve over asphalt, weave over lines. I duck streetlights that are only six feet tall.

Man, I *missed* this.

This feeling of getting your speed up and making it work for you. There's nothing like it. Nothing at all. If you've pushed yourself, you know it. If you haven't, you don't. Simple.

Little Nate takes up a position down the little road a piece, thinks better of it, and moves to where he has an angle on Kurtis coming up the road and me going up onto the building like it's an up ramp, biking to the top, having a pause on the topmost point of it, and then blazing down the back slope, picking up speed, and jumping off just a few feet before landing safely.

It was only about half-effort from me. I needed to feel how far that took me.

As I get ready to do a full-speed run the next time, Akil and Kurtis get Kurtis's bike parked and kickstanded up right in the road where I'll be jumping. It goes like the time before. I get up some speed, pop up onto the roof, grind hard on the up slope, and then pump my legs on the way down.

When I hit the edge and wheelie off, I clear the bike by a good foot or more.

I know it's that good because Kurtis and Akil do some quiet celebrating with chuckles and low fives. I tell them I need the bike closer, though, a foot closer to the little lip of the building so I'm hitting the top of my jump above it and not coming down over it. We test back and forth a bit to try to get the timing right. We time it both ways. We see how long it takes me to hit the down slope so Kurtis knows how fast to go, and then we try it for real.

We do four takes for Little Nate.

The first one Kurtis goes too fast and isn't there when I jump. The second one he goes too slow. The third one he gets right but I abort because I feel my back wheel slide a bit so I just drop down safely rather than risk it.

The fourth time is the charm, though.

I hit the lip so right that I actually take time to look down as I cruise right over Kurtis going perpendicular underneath me, leaning flat with his back stretched out the length of his seat, his shins tucked up under the handlebars, keeping the bike straight.

We lock eyes as I'm in the air and he points his chin at me.

And I don't know how I know what he wants to do. It just happens. I just know that he's going to put his right hand up, so I take mine off the bars as I'm flying and I reach down as he moves his leg to steady the bike so he can reach up with his right hand and then *bam*, we slap palms in an almost perfect five if it didn't catch only about half of my hand.

Behind us, I hear Akil scream, "oh shit!" as I land, wobble, and hold it. And that's that, I guess. We might not be a pack, but we are a team.

A good one too.

"Yo," Little Nate says as he's watching playback on the back of his camera and kind of talking to himself, "I can't wait to see what people think of *this*."

23

WHAT PEOPLE THINK

We rode for about twenty-two more minutes. Little Nate had a timer on his camera, so that's how we know so specifically, because he shot the whole dang time nonstop. We pulled more tricks and stuff but nothing so crazy as an improvised midair high five from bike to dirt bike. Twenty-two minutes is how long it took for two Druid Hill Park janitors to roll through in these tiny little garbage trucks (a third of the size of a real one and with only room for one person to drive) and tell us to get the hell out or they'd get the cops on us.

As Akil says the next day at Kurtis's, "If they'd been white, there's no way they'd've given us a warning like that. If they'd seen us from a distance, the phone just gets a dial and rings on the other end at the police station."

Akil's probably right. The men stopped their trucks right

by the gate, got out, and came at us like concerned uncles, but maybe I'm thinking that because one of them looked an awful lot like my Aunt Judy's boyfriend, Jim. He's not my uncle, but he's my uncle. They've been together as long as I've been alive, just never got married. I don't know why. Anyways, Jim's tall like basketball players but he never played a day in his life, and he's got this hangdog face (that's what Grandpa calls it) that always makes it look like he feels sorry for you. At Momma's funeral though, I don't think he was faking it. I don't think anyone was.

So these janitors came at us and explained in some loud, firm voices how we never should've done this and we need to get the heck out. Their eyes weren't in it, though.

You could tell. It hadn't even crossed my mind how different the interaction would've gone if they'd been white.

"I'm not saying you're wrong, Keel"—Kurtis says *Akil* like it's got one syllable in it—"but how many white janitors you know round here?"

Akil tilts his head at that. He's running numbers. Not coming up with much. "None," he finally says, "but there's got to be some. Like maybe around Locust Point or something, when the factories were still kicking?"

"Doubt it," Kurtis says. "Brothers did the bad work, even back then."

Nobody fights that statement. Nobody fights most things Kurtis says, but that one just seems to make sense so we take it as truth. The thought of someone talking back to Kurtis reminds me we haven't seen Darryl since that one night we met. I think we replaced him somehow, me and Akil, at least until we screw up too, and that's a weird feeling. But a good feeling too. For the first time since I've been in Baltimore, I feel on the inside of something. And as I'm feeling the warmth of it, I do something stupid. I ask where Mon is.

"Why you asking?"

Akil looks at me like, *don't you* ever *ask about another man's girl, dummy!*

And I see that and know I screwed up before I say, "I dunno. She just seemed like the queen bee around here is all."

Akil's eyes go even wider. He wants me to shut up. Now. Cut my losses.

Seems Kurtis does too, because he says, "Only thing you need to care about 'around here' is the king bee."

"My bad," I say. "You're right."

I try to leave it at that. I go over to Kurtis's bookcase and browse it again. I'm noticing now how there's not a single new spine among them. They've all been read, whether by Kurtis or a previous owner, I don't know. Kurtis follows me over.

He nods his chin at me. "Did I scare you or what?"

"No," I say, but I make a face like maybe.

What I can't say is *he* didn't scare me, what scared me was the possibility of me saying something stupid and screwing all this up. Me. Akil. Kurtis. Because it's like a dream come true right now, hanging out like this, and I don't want to ruin it.

"Ha. I *did* get you!" Kurtis barks a laugh. "I'm just playing!"

Somewhere in that tone though, there's still a warning. He's playing, but like ninety-five percent playing. The rest is real serious. "You read much?"

"Yeah," I say. "A little."

"What're you reading now?"

I run my finger over the spines vertically, feeling the long grooves that have been worked into them.

"I'm finishing up *Invisible Man*," I lie. "Got a couple chapters left."

I'm still where I was before, not even cracking Chapter Six.

"Wells or Ellison?" Kurtis sounds impressed.

I didn't know the other name and didn't want him to know that I didn't, so I just say, "Ellison."

"Damn," he says, and looks even more impressed. "What's your favorite part?"

"I think the prologue," I say.

He makes a face like no one in the history of the world has ever said the prologue, and then he asks me why.

"Well," I say, "because it starts at the end, sort of. He knew he needed to be visible, but the only way to make that leap was to realize first he was invisible."

Kurtis thinks about that before answering.

"I mean, realizations are all good, as you say, but you can never be great just thinking anything. Eventually you've got to stand up and do something about it. Action's the only way." He starts bouncing up and down a little as he says it. "That can be riding, or jumping, or whatever. But it's got to be *something* in motion. Something moving. It's got to be doing. Philosophy in action is way more than just that. It becomes contagious so long as it's true."

Contagious. I've never thought of it that way before.

This conversation must've sparked something for Akil, because right then he cuts in with, "So when are we gonna see what Little Nate shot the other day?"

Kurtis laughs. "See it? Like run it by you first so you can put a director's cut on it? Approve it and all that?"

Akil looks at me and I look at him before saying, "Not really."

"You're damn right *not really.* That shit's already up on the MeTube anyway."

"Huh?" That's me and Akil both, at the same time.

"That's YouTube," Kurtis says through a smile. "But whenever I get put up there, it becomes MeTube. Little Nate did it last night."

Kurtis moves over to the computer and flicks at the mouse. That wakes his screen up. His desktop background is a photo of him doing a Superman on a dirt bike.

That's when you ride on one wheel, balancing your back foot on the end of the seat, and ride your bike straight up like you're windsurfing or something. It's impressive how relaxed he looks. And judging by the blur on the image background, he must be going real, real fast.

Kurtis covers that up with a browser window, though. It's already pointed at a YouTube page with a title ("Introducing

Air") above a big black rectangle stuck on pause.

"What's that mean," I say, "'Introducing Air'?"

"That's you," Kurtis says to me.

"But I'm Grey."

"First off, don't nobody need to know your real name. You think Kurtis is mine?"

It's a little confusing for a moment, but it feels all right that Kurtis thinks Grey's my real name, because it feels like my real name now, but then I think, *Why wouldn't he?*

I've never been introduced as anything different.

And I'm hesitant to say so, but I feel compelled to tell Kurtis the truth about how I thought it was his real name.

"Yeah," I say. "I did."

"Man, not even close. I took it from that old school rapper, Kurtis Blow." He looks at me like I might know who that is, but I don't.

"Never mind," he says. "Look it up later. You just need to face up to it. Grey is what you were, but Air is what you *are*. It's how you transcend."

I feel stupid even asking, but I have to. "What's that mean, *transcend*?"

Kurtis isn't weird about it or anything. He doesn't look at me funny like some teachers might (especially Mr. Russell, my civics & American history teacher who makes a sour face every time you ask a question). Kurtis doesn't take this as an opportunity to talk down to me. And the look on Akil's face even shows me he's glad I asked, because he wants to know too.

"It's how you go beyond what you got," Kurtis says. "It's how you become something more than just skin and bones. It's a launching pad."

Man, I *like* that. It's got me nodding along with it almost like it's a song. And that's that too. I've got a new name now. *Air.*

It's me and it's more than me at the same time.

I can't really soak this in though, because Akil's leaning past me, pointing at the screen.

"Guess one of the benefits of being up on Kurtis's channel is instant audience. Check this out, we got comments already," he says, picking one out and reading it out loud. "'That fives shit was cheesy, son.' Wow. Haters *will* hate."

"But did you see the reply to it though?" I read it out. "'You try doing that shit, dummy. So many moving parts I bet you fucking die.'"

It didn't really say *fucking*. It said *f&^%ing*. But that was what was meant. The rest of the comments are more positive than negative. Crazy positive.

"True. And look how many thumbs-down that first one got—see right here?" Kurtis gets a fingertip real close to the computer screen and static *pop-pop*s. "Six. And look how many thumbs-up the reply got. Nineteen."

"It's like a *scoreboard*," Akil says. "You can see who's winning."

"Yes and no," Kurtis says, and since he's the king of this, you know we're listening hard. "On comments and whatnot, you mostly see waves of opinion. Some stupid as hell, some not, and then how they agree or disagree with each other. But I mean, big picture, sure, it's about views. And me and Wheelie Wayne been battling back and forth for King of B-more on that for a while now. He was first to a million views, though, got to give him that. But I have more million-view videos than he does. Like I said, he does his thing, and I do mine. It's not always apples to apples, you know? Because when we post me jumping off a damn building, it's a whole new game."

"Hold up," Akil says, "you got video of that?"

The jumping thing he did never made the news, if you can believe it. The biggest mention of it in the *Sun* was just that traffic was disturbed by "renegade bikers," but it didn't say why.

Kurtis doesn't even say anything back to Akil. He just smiles with the right side of his mouth crooking up and nods with it all slow and then he clicks PLAY on our Safety City video, and the rectangle springs to life with a picture of me BMXing in slow motion, and I shiver right then.

I shiver all over. Watching myself on the screen feels like an out-of-body experience. Like it's me and not-me doing that jump. I point at the screen like an idiot. Can't help it.

"It almost seems like it's some other rider there," I say.

But I still have the memory of it. My stomach remembers how it felt.

Kurtis laughs. "I remember that feeling. But it's good to know what your style looks from the outside in. It's important to know how you look when you doing what you doing. One you get that, you can captivate."

The word explodes in my head like a firework. *Captivate.*

24

A CERTAIN WAY

There did end up being a press conference a couple days after
Kurtis's base jump, though. One with the mayor in it. I guess
that's what you get for jumping six blocks from police head-
quarters and then getting away on dirt bikes. There's got to be a
response. And this one was the mayor saying he was creating a
special community-outreach task force to deal with the scourge
of urban biking. *Scourge of urban biking.* That's a direct quote.

He said that on live TV.

But what was most interesting about the whole thing was a
line of police officers behind the mayor. And one guy stood out.
Three to the right. Bald. Muscled. Face squished together like
his momma fed him lemons when he was little and he never
stopped puckering so his face sort of grew around it. As soon as
I saw him, I knew it was Cogland. I got a real good look at him,

and I saw what Akil meant when he said he was all forehead. The whole time the thing was being explained, Cogland looked real serious.

Apparently, this task force is all set up to "prevent youth from motorbiking in urban areas." That's a quote. They didn't add *black* to that, but it's pretty obvious they're not talking about white kids when they say it. The task force is called Policing Our Safe Streets Effectively, and the acronym to that is P.O.S.S.E. Like it's the Wild West or something.

And I'm wondering what Akil and Kurtis will think about that as I push a cart through Giant Food for Aunt Blue. We're grocery shopping for the week. It's a new thing we have to do together since I didn't come home until dawn that one night. It's a punishment, I guess, but it doesn't feel like a bad one. She actually lets me pick out stuff I want for lunch and dinner, so it's not bad.

I haven't told her about the Safety City video. I haven't had to. Nothing bad's happened from it yet. I wonder what will happen if she ever sees it, though. Maybe I won't get in trouble for it since I'm only BMXing. I hope so anyway.

My biking just doesn't really get talked about anymore. Not since that night. My grades are the same, holding steady. I even put some big fat A's on some tests I was working hard for. I made sure to bring those home and put them on the fridge myself.

Aunt Blue didn't get elated or anything. She just said it was expected, and besides, she cares about something else too.

She starts in on me in the produce aisle, by the carrot dis-play that's almost as tall as me. She says, "You finished reading *Invisible Man* yet? I noticed your bookmark's not moved in a few days."

"No, ma'am," I say. "It hasn't and I've not."

"You got two days, young man."

"I know," I say. "It'll get finished."

We move out of produce and into the deli. Aunt Blue scans sliced cheeses to find something right for sandwiches. She picks up two packages, one in each hand. Cheddar for her left and American for her right. She says, "You got any opinions so far?"

But she's not talking about cheese. She's still on the book.

"Not really," I say. "Just that maybe I know what it's like."

She puts the cheddar back on its hook and turns to give me the eye. The one where I feel it weighing me up in every way.

She says, "What *what's* like?"

I stop the cart and say, "The invisibility thing."

She makes a face first before she says anything. It's like a smirk.

"Oh you do, *do* you?" Her tone's heavy when she says it, like she's about to drop some knowledge on me.

That's because she thinks I'm being young and stupid to pre-sume that life in the twenty-first century can even come close to the difficulties of being black when Ellison wrote. I can hear it in her voice. And the thing is, I'm not disagreeing with that. I know I can't ever really understand what people like Grandpa went through. But what I need to say is just that I understand invisibility in a different way—in a new way, maybe.

"Before I felt like I'm always one thing or the other," I say, trying to get in front of her train of thought before it steamrolls me. "Not enough black or not enough white depending on who I'm talking to. But the thing is, I don't know how to feel like one or the other. I'll always feel like both. I can't change being grey, but that doesn't stop people from seeing me a certain way." I get us going again, back toward the front of the store since we're done with our list, but I don't stop talking. I keep going. "So it's like that, I guess. I'm used to not being seen for all of who I am. People see me from the angle they want to see me, and that depends on how they've been raised and where they're coming from and what their own beliefs are."

Her body language changes a lot when I say that last bit. Her spine gets looser.

She relaxes down off her soapbox and just nods like maybe I have a point. We walk down the rest of the aisle with the refrigerators humming their soft hum around yogurt and lunch meat as we make our way to the registers. It's standing in line there that she makes sure to mention that Maryland people do it right when she points up at the 15 ITEMS OR FEWER sign for one of the express lanes.

"That's grammatically correct right there," she says. "You ever see 'fifteen items or less,' you know it's wrong. *Fewer* is for items that can be counted. It's the same for people too. They're never less. Only fewer. People can be counted too, you know."

I feel like there's a lesson in there somewhere, but I can't unravel it yet, so I don't say anything.

When we get home there's a package in the mail for me from the state department of motor vehicles. It's longer than an average envelope, a little heavy, and not bendable. I already know what it is. It's a Maryland motorcycle license plate with a registration sticker and a date-of-expiration sticker.

This license plate, it was a gift and it wasn't. I mean, she's too smart, Aunt Blue.

She knew she couldn't take the bike away from me if it was Akil's. So she gave me some allowance for the chores I've been doing (scraping out gutters on weekends, picking up the basement, spraying wood stuff on all the furniture and wiping it off, doing dishes, doing ironing) and encouraged me to buy it off him on a payment plan. I'm halfway through one and Akil loves getting paid weekly.

I'm not so sure about it, though. Because all of this was less a way for my aunt to say, *I believe in you*, and more to say, *you better be responsible but if you screw up, you know what's happening*. Besides, with a plate, I'm registered, and if I can get a ticket, she can take the bike away then too. The whole thing is her way of enlisting other people (the state, the cops) in keeping me accountable and what she thinks is safe. It's hard not to respect how she's played this whole thing. She still hates that I do it. She still makes faces if I ever mention it. But she's being real strategic, like she's just waiting for it to go boom in my face so she can swoop in and say, *I told you so!*

"Look at you, all legal," she says, crowing a little.

"Yeah," I say.

I set the plate on the kitchen table so I can finish loading the groceries into the fridge. She says, "Are you ready for your appointment?"

Right after she says it, Aunt Blue jingles her car keys.

And when I hear that sound I get a cold sweat in an instant, and I figure this must be how it feels for animals to have to go to the vet, because Aunt Blue aims to drive me to the psychologist right now. And I don't want to go, but I have to.

I promised. It's a price I have to pay.

25

TOP IT

Me and Akil are sitting on nonmoving bikes in Kurtis's open garage while Kurtis rummages around on his tool bench for something to fix a leaking master cylinder on his bike. Little Nate's out on the driveway in a lawn chair, getting some sun on his face. It's late afternoon, not raining, but threatening to. The whole sky's full of different banks of clouds mashing into each other. Some sun pokes through, and it's hitting the driveway now, but the rest of the sky looks like a bumpy forehead, like maybe it's mad at the earth.

Behind us, we hear the little *whish* sounds of cars going by on the other side of the house, but it's a longer sound than that, like the word has about twelve *i*'s in it, because as cars swing toward us on the curve and then roll away, the sound comes toward and then fades. Toward and then fades.

I'm holding the license plate in my hands. It already has the stickers on it.

"Is there a way to put this on and off quick? On for my aunt. Off when I'm on the streets?"

Screwing it in and out of the little frame Aunt Blue bought me to go with it would never work. It'd take too much time.

"Magnets," Akil says.

Kurtis doesn't look up from his tool bench. "Prolly not, Keel. You hit one good bump, that thing's dropping off, and if you're up to no good at the time, you just handed the knockos all your information."

Knockos is another name for cops, at least in Baltimore. I don't know why. I haven't had the courage to ask yet. If I ask, it's just another thing that makes me an outsider. And if I've learned anything about life since being here it's that only two things can ever make you an insider: time and knowledge.

Well, maybe trust too. And it's weird to have that and not the other two.

Sometimes it feels like I'm always playing catch-up.

"Yeah," Little Nate says, "And if knockos got your info, you know P.O.S.S.E. shows up at your house the next day."

Kurtis sniffs.

"Yeah. They're calling it community outreach and education now but just you watch, if they forming a posse, then we'll definitely end up being the bad guys. Believe that." Kurtis looks at each one of us in turn and waits for that to sink in before getting back to the matter at hand. "I think you need a bracket or something that can pinch it like a little metal crab claw, hold it nice and tight. Maybe four. One for each corner."

"Could work," Akil says. "If you find something that gets it tight enough."

It sounds like it'd take a lot of work to figure that out. I make a promise to myself right then that I'll only be putting the plate on if Aunt Blue makes me. But my brain's already churning on something else, on the prospect of being a bad guy. A villain. I don't feel like one, but maybe that's what all bad guys think? I mean, I've heard how some gangs around use dirt bikes to move drugs. To do drive-bys. Whatever. But that's not us. We're trying to be free of all that. Trying to transcend.

I don't know what Akil or Kurtis are thinking about, but maybe it's the same thing. We're all kind of quiet, looking down and processing, when Little Nate decides it must be up to him to change the course of the conversation. "Anybody see how that Safety City video's doing?"

"You know what I see," Kurtis says. "A black man taking sun. What's a brother as dark as you doing that for anyways? You know you ain't gonna tan."

Me and Akil cover our mouths to keep from laughing.

"I like how it feels," Little Nate says. "I'm getting my vitamin D up!"

"Big as you is, you look like you get more vitamins than all four of us combined."

"Ha-ha, bish. I might be fat, but you're the most unoriginal comedian ever. So stop trying to change the subject."

Bish is how Little Nate says *bitch*. I don't know why that is either. To ask why is to risk being called one, so I mostly just listen and try to learn.

"Shit has gone viral. It's spreading like crazy."

Everybody's listening now. Even Kurtis.

Kurtis asks what we all want to know. "How viral?"

"None of y'all checked?" Little Nate's voice is going so high, it sounds like his head's about to pop off. "Really? It's been a week and it's multiplying views every day."

I don't even ask what that means.

"In fact," Little Nate adds, "it even got featured on one of those Internet video TV shows on cable. It got real crazy then. Comments up, likes up. Everything. It's got the highest engagement we've ever had, and that's saying something."

It's out of my mouth before I realize how stupid it sounds. "There's TV shows about online videos?"

"Boy," Akil says, "the shit you don't know could fill every library there ever was."

He adds a punch to the arm as end punctuation too. But it's not too hard.

"Makes sense," Kurtis says. "Nothing prettier than a black kid riding his BMX bicycle. Don't see much of that around."

Kurtis smiles at me. I shrug my shoulders like, *it was an okay stunt, but thanks.*

I'm thinking about his language, though. How once again I'm one or the other. I'm black, not white. Once again, I'm not both to anybody. But here, in this garage, that's not bad. It actually means I belong. It means we're the same. Being black with Kurtis is almost like graduating from mixed.

And I'll take that.

"It means we got to top it next time though. Gotta be bigger and badder. Push the envelope." Little Nate folds his lawn chair up and stashes it just inside the garage door. "And that means planning."

Kurtis follows him inside the house, but Akil and I stay out, at least for a minute. "Hey," Akil says now that we're alone, "how'd that meeting with the doctor go?" This is what I get for telling Akil about the psychologist—Dr. Vereen, her name is.

"I guess it went all right."

"What's that mean, 'all right,' and why're you guessing?"

All right means I cried. It snuck up on me. I didn't even mean to. It was ugly too. Sniffles and mucus and sobs. Stuff I couldn't even control. Body shakes. All because she told me to close my eyes and tell what I saw about how Momma died. She made me tell her step-by-step. Where I was that day. What the weather was like. How it felt when I saw. I tried real hard, but I couldn't get past my dad's face when I told. I couldn't get past the look on it. Dr. Vereen said that was okay. She said I could try again next time.

I tell Akil, "I don't want to talk about it."

"Okay." Akil's nodding at me like I'm hiding something from him that I shouldn't be, that we're brothers now that our moms are dead, and he doesn't like me being silent about trying to heal. I'm supposed to share it. I'm supposed to help him too.

He's jealous, a little, about me having an aunt that cares, but he'll never say it.

I know he puts all his pain into riding. Being on two wheels is his therapy. It's kind of been mine too.

And I don't want to lose that.

But maybe if I keep going, keep trying, and make what happened to my momma a story, then my riding will become something else.

What that is though, I don't know.

26

TO PROTECT AND SERVE

Since I've been going there, we've never had an assembly at City where knockos came, showed us pictures of road accidents involving dirt bikers, and waited for us outside the school afterward to hand out pamphlets on road safety, but I guess this is what the education part of P.O.S.S.E. was supposed to be about. This was the outreach. And it felt like a punch in the stomach.

I had to sit around for forty-five minutes at the end of the school day and listen to them talk about the *scourge* of dirt biking *plaguing* Baltimore—man, they used heavy words, but hearing them was good, because it taught me that words are part of the fight too, convincing people to your side means you need an angle—and the whole time I'm sitting there thinking about that, I got this sinking feeling knowing they were talking about me. And Akil. And Kurtis. And basically I just got mad and wanted to yell at Cogland standing up there acting all righteous about public safety when he put people in danger all the time. But Cogland wasn't the only one talking. There were three others. I didn't catch the names of two of them, but Leonard was there too. Leonard loved his nightstick. Everybody knows that. There's a story going around about that one time he managed to wedge the thing into somebody's spokes, wiped them out, picked up his stick, and left.

They were talking, but they were paying attention to us too, making eye contact, and maybe looking at faces. And that was when I knew there was a downside to being visible, of deciding not to wear a helmet or even a mask when I rode and took video and posted it so anybody could see it. That anybody includes cops. I knew that, but I didn't know it this good until sitting there in the auditorium with all the lights on, at the very back, watching them watch the crowd. The education thing made a messed-up kind of sense. If they convinced a few more people dirt bikes were awful, it was a win, but it sure seemed to me like they were trying to see if they could identify anybody. It was tactical. And it didn't stop there either.

If I could've gone out another exit other than the main one, I would have, but teachers herded us out the main exit and its pale stone arch that has THE BALTIMORE CITY COLLEGE, FOUNDED 1839 carved into it in the craziest calligraphy letters. There's this strip of asphalt right outside there that butts up to the building, and it gets used like a road sometimes. Staff in the office will drive their cars up and park them there if they're loading stuff in or out, but today there are two cop cars parked there, diagonally, with their noses pointed at the doors. It's aggressive, is what it is.

Behind the cars are the four cops, fanned out in a semicircle, to catch students trying to go all directions so they can press pamphlets into their hands. And I turn to my left because Leonard's in front of me and when I see Cogland's the guy in front of me then, I curse myself but I just have to go with it.

He doesn't look as bad now as he did on TV. His face isn't quite as scrunched up, and he's bigger than me by a lot. A few inches. Thirty pounds. He's still bald. He also has a scar on his jaw up near the socket. As I'm eyeing that, Cogland sees me and actually takes a step forward, and then two. He's heading right straight toward me like he's been waiting for me. He's got a look in his eye like he recognizes me and that twists my guts up inside me.

I go over my options. I can run, I can stop, or I can keep walking toward the bus stop. I decide not to do any of them. I walk right up to him, which throws him a little. He definitely didn't think I'd do that, and I'm glad.

We look at each other for a moment when we get face-to-face, not like a duel or anything, but just like, *oh, that's who you are*. He's seen me in a video. I've heard about him in stories and seen him on TV.

"Officer Cogland," I say, "thanks for your time and presentation today."

Aunt Blue always says when you talk to policemen as a young black man you've got to A.B.P. Always be polite. It throws them.

And it throws Cogland too. He smiles a half-smile that goes away faster than it came. He says, "It's a fact of life in Baltimore that bad things happen out on these streets. Don't they, Air?"

"I'm sorry, officer. I don't know anyone by that name."

"Yeah, well, I know you. And I know you're not from around here because you sure don't talk like it." He steps to the side of me then, and I jerk a little, but he's just moving so he can look where I'm looking, at the big old City building that looks like a cross between a church and a factory. "I know you go here."

I look to the tennis courts down the hill, like they're going to rescue me or something. They're not.

Students stream by around us, some looking at me and wondering why I'm talking to a knocko, or why a knocko's talking to me. I don't know if any of them know I'm Air. I don't care either.

I lean in toward Cogland and say something I heard Mon telling Akil when he asked about getting arrested for being on a video, because I'm starting to panic, but a quiet panic that I make sure doesn't reach my voice, "You can't arrest me off of a riding video. A misdemeanor—and it undoubtedly would be a misdemeanor—requires an officer's presence at the scene. Now, if no officer was there and you get a witness to that wrongdoing later, you need a statement sworn out to a commissioner and then that person needs to find probable cause to issue a summons to give to you, the officer, before you can scoop me up. I mean, I *think* that's how it goes. Isn't it?"

In that same conversation I found out Mon's studying to be a paralegal now, and a lawyer later. She'll do it. She's as smart as it gets. And I must be looking at least a little smug at repeating her words because Cogland's back goes straighter.

He says, "You think you're pretty smart, don't you? I can arrest you wherever and whenever I want." Cogland wipes his mouth like he's thinking. "Do you even know what public safety is?"

"Yeah," I say.

"Go on then," he says, like a challenge.

"Safety is the deepest defensive position on a football field." I do my best Little Nate I-just-got-over-on-you-while-you-were-trying-be-serious grin.

Cogland grimaces at that. "It's no joke. Safety is a condition of being protected from unnecessary danger or risk—that's what safety is, a *condition*. You see that motto?"

He points to the door of the police car. *To Protect and Serve.* I don't say anything. He doesn't need me to.

"That's what I signed up for. Now, when you do what you do on some dirt road in the middle of nowhere, you only put yourself at risk, and that's okay by me, because you're free to do that." Cogland steps back in front of me then, leans in, stares me dead in the eyes, and hisses at me. "But when you do it in public, you put others at risk. Innocent people! You think riding is just being fun and free? No. When you do it the way you do it, on public streets, you destroy that condition of safety for other people. And that is not acceptable to me. That little girl getting her foot run over by a bike in Edmundson Hill and needing it amputated—that is not acceptable to me or any other good citizen. So that's where I come in. I'm the protection. And if you're out of control, I need to protect other people from *you*."

I'm scared. I can't even lie. But I turn that energy into something else when I say, "How many times have you practiced that speech?"

That makes him mad. I watch his eyes go wide, then narrow, and he says, "Your freedom can't come at somebody else's expense. If it does, it's not free. Somebody's paying. Do you *get* that?"

"Are you gonna break my wrists and ankles so I can't ride?"

He looks genuinely surprised. "Boy, where'd even you hear that?"

"I'm not a boy," I say as calm as I can. "You saying it's not true?"

He eyes me up.

"You're right. I'm sorry about that. You're not a boy. Tell me this, though. Why do you even do it? You got a real chance here to make something of yourself." He nods at the school, and he sounds real sincere, and I don't totally know how to process that. "Don't let yourself get dragged down. You can be so much more than Air."

He hands me a pamphlet and I take it as he's turning away. The flow of students has slowed to a trickle, but he still finds another one to hand a pamphlet to, and I just stare at his back for a second before heading for the bus stop.

27

AIR'S BEEN BORN

It's a Wednesday night, Aunt Blue's on a seven-to-seven night shift again, and this time, to avoid ever getting home too late, I've set a little alarm on my watch to pop at two in the morning just to make certain I'm home and sleeping for a few hours before she gets in. This is extra important because we had a difficult talk in the morning about me holding up my end. I lied and told her yes. It was the only way to keep going out.

When I took the pamphlet over to Kurtis's, nobody could quite believe it was real.

This regular piece of paper folded three ways with stats (number of accidents involving bikes in Baltimore) and pictures (of victims) was real, though, and smart too. On the back, there was a special number for people to call to report dirt bikers. Nobody liked that, but Kurtis wasn't too worried.

After that, we all tripped on Cogland knowing me by sight and where I go to school now. They wanted to know what he was like in person.

"Before," I said, "I thought he was a villain that just didn't care about anybody, but talking to him, he seemed like a real person. Sincere. Human, I guess. He definitely believes in what he's doing."

"And how do you know," Akil says, "that he wasn't putting that on to fool you? Especially if he recognized you! Anybody can fake caring."

"I don't know," I say, playing it off a little. "It didn't seem fake. He just has his priorities, and that's safety above everything. Safety for everybody. And maybe he's just willing to do anything to get that."

"That's stupid." Kurtis had a look on his face like I just said the worst thing ever said. "Who the hell ever got free being *safe*? What we need to do is hit back!"

After a living room powwow, it got decided we'd be going downtown, to the Inner Harbor. Little Nate suggested it. He thought it'd be the riskiest, the coolest.

Definitely the best way to get back at P.O.S.S.E. and their pamphlets. Akil said he wasn't so sure, but Kurtis overruled him. He said there was a spot down there that I could probably BMX real good.

Little Nate leaves first. He drives the van Darryl took last time. He puts my BMX in it so I don't have to ride with it. His mission is to get downtown, find a good spot, and roll over to the park nearby the Inner Harbor—across the street from it—and bring my bike. He leaves an hour before us.

o   o   o

It's long past dark when me, Akil, and Kurtis get ready to roll out. "I'm still not liking the risk/reward on this," Akil says.

"Got to get outside this fishbowl somehow, though," Kurtis says, flashing that smile of his that could convince water not to be wet. "Might as well be tonight. Got to be showing them something. Pushing is what we do. It's who we are. Besides, even if the knockos pop up on us, they can't chase. And we'll lose them in the one-ways."

Akil shrugs and smiles. "If it's got to be done, it gets done."

But I can tell he's a little nervous. I think he wants to put on the right front, though, and make sure nobody thinks he's scared to do it. Don't get me wrong, though, I'm scared, and I've definitely heard stories about cops chasing when they're not supposed to, of them causing accidents and leaving riders broken on the pavement. I think of Evander Brycewell then, of how terrible it must have been to have to wait for that ambulance and not even last to hear the sirens.

But we go.

We go because we can't not. Because we'd follow Kurtis anywhere and he knows it. And maybe he's taking advantage of it when he starts his engine and leads us out of the driveway, but trust is a two-way street, and if he trusts me, then I have to trust him too.

We go from Hilldale to Druid Park, our engines telling the neighborhood to either wake up or ignore us. Before we even get to Reisterstown Road, kids come out of nowhere. They materialize from row homes and follow us. These late-night kids, flowing like ghosts in the wind. Some don't have shirts on, looking like they just rolled out of bed. Some run along the sidewalk, shouting out *Kurtis*. And that's nothing new, I've seen that before, but something new happens that throws me off.

They recognize me.

"Hey, it's Air," they shout. "Hey, *Air!*"

It feels like my whole life is changing. Almost like I can feel it split in two somehow, like—like a new me got created when I hadn't even meant to, but it was here now. Air was real. Little kids were chanting it at me like it meant something other than what they were breathing. They're riding hard behind us on bicycles, pumping their little legs as fast as they'll go, and still falling behind. Groups of twos and threes are jumping up and down on sidewalks like it's a concert or something.

I turn to look at the riders behind me, three in a little pack, wobbling and streaking forward together—trying not to hit each other but trying to go fast—and when I do, they cheer. They stand on their pedals. They lean back and scream.

I've never felt anything like it in my whole life. I feel their cheers like a hot blanket all over my body. It's hugging me. It's stifling. It's more than that.

They see me, I think. *Air's been born.*

And it tingles in my fingers, daring me to go faster, to go harder, so I do. I crank the gas.

I accelerate.

28

INNER HARBOR

All the way downtown, I'm still thinking about being Air. How maybe it's better than Air Jordan because it's just one word like Eminem. And then I'm thinking that's good because I don't want anyone thinking I ripped it off from the shoes. Just hearing it, no one's going to know I got named it. That Kurtis did it. Names aren't always attached like that unless you're a Junior and then people know where it came from. And that one I know too well. It seems like most all names have histories, but we have to tell them to people. Only if we want to. I haven't told Akil or Kurtis why I'm called Grey yet. I don't know why. It's never really come up, I guess. It's just accepted. And I like that.

Akil told me once what the Inner Harbor was all about: money. Tourists and their money. But mostly money. Ten-dollar ice cream. Staring at boats. U.S.S. *Constitution*. Or maybe he said *Constellation*. There's a submarine parked there too. I think he said it has a face painted on it. It sits on top of the water in front of an aquarium. Inside there, they have sharks. But they only have them because they can charge for you to look, and it all comes back to money.

Now, I'm new to this, but even I know that to this point, dudes have been riding up on Druid Hill for a few years easy. They ride in big groups, mostly not hurting anybody, maybe scaring people, maybe being loud, maybe being reckless sometimes, and I'm not excusing it, just saying it is what it is. It's become something. A culture.

But that was forged in a neighborhood that isn't all white, Akil said. Around where Kurtis lives, it's mixed. Working black folks and white union men. Some Mexicans too. I guess I'm saying there's more leeway up around the park, but maybe not because of race. Because it's poorer. But here? Inner Harbor surrounded by new buildings and restaurants? Man, they *pay* people to clean sidewalks around here. And knowing that, I don't think they'll let us get away with anything. I think they're happy for us to ride where most of the people we're disturbing aren't white. But here, this is different. Cops'll be on us quick.

I don't even need to wonder if that's why Kurtis dragged us here. I know. Seeing his face like he's the general of an invading army. Chin up. Small smile.

He's sitting real tall in his seat, back completely straight, like he's surveying a battlefield and he already knows he's gonna win.

But me, I'm not so sure.

Hit and get out, I'm thinking. *We need to hit and get the hell out.*

As we get to Light Street and bang a right from Pratt, I see Little Nate standing in this park on the outer horseshoe of the harbor. I'm getting a bad feeling. It's like an I-just-ate-a-bad-piece-of-fish feeling. I try to look to Akil to see if he shares it too, but he's not looking at me. He's looking at a fountain.

McKeldin, that's what it's called. It's our target.

I push the bad feeling down inside me then, because it doesn't do to be nagging anybody about anything. It won't change where we are, and it might make me look weak and scared, which I'm *not*. I just have a bad feeling as I roll up onto the park's grass, cut my engine, brake to a stop at the base of the stairs, kick my stand, and lean it.

Hit and get out.

My BMX is waiting at the bottom there, so I keep my momentum going and I just grab it. I'm running up the stairs with it on my shoulder. I stop on the first landing, though. I've never really looked at what they want me to ride before. Not even in pictures or daylight. And that's another bad thing. They're stacking up now.

It's all concrete and angles, this thing. Squares on top of squares. There's turquoise paint where the water sits in big square basins. At least it looks turquoise in the dark. That brownish Colorado turquoise with little ripples of copper-black through it.

That kind. The whole thing reminds me of the polar bear enclosure at the Denver Zoo.

"Do that Air thing you do," Kurtis says with a wide white smile I can see even in the dark.

And it's not like that short-circuits my bad feelings, but it pushes them back, because that's Kurtis's power. You want to make him happy. You want to impress him. You want to make him proud. I do, anyway.

So I get up to the top and test the rails with my hand as Little Nate pops this light on his camera and it's like a spotlight in his hand, it's so bright. Just moving it over the concrete throws all kinds of shadows. Black rectangles shudder and move when he does.

I haven't ridden rails in a while, but these are wide. Six inches. That's not a tightrope, that's like a little bridge. Twice as wide as my tire. Still, though. I'm not about to jump on to this. That's just not happening. So I lean my BMX beside me and climb up onto the rail before hoisting it up, getting it square and balanced, pointing down toward where Akil is.

He hasn't even dismounted. He's still on his bike. Ready to ride at a moment's notice. I don't blame him. He's close enough to Little Nate's camera that I can see his face in the light. He looks more nervous than before.

I don't like seeing that so I think I just need to go. I push off and take the rail straight and then down a slope to the next landing, which is straight again, and then down and I pull a little pop-off. That's what I call it when I ollie off the end of it.

So that's what I do, as I'm rolling down the angle, I tense my whole body and try to jump with the bike as I'm getting to the end of the rail.

And I pop off okay, but I don't get the height I'm looking for because I didn't time it right. I was pulling up as my weight was already leaving the rail, so it just ended up being this lame, little jump at the end.

I land well, only a little wobbly, and I hop off and go back to the top and do it all again. The second pop-off's a little better but I'm missing the end lip and not getting any height, definitely not enough to flip, which is what Kurtis wants me to do. It was discussed in the garage as the only way to top Safety City.

I go back to the top and hit one more, and this time it's good but not high enough, and as I'm thinking I can possibly pull off a flip, I see a crowd gathering. With the light on me, I can't make out what they look like. I can't see for the brightness, but there's a few of them. Five or six.

I'm breathing heavy as I get up on top of the rail again. My transitions from down slope to flat could be better, so as I get going down the first angle, I tense myself up good as the wind dances around my ears and I curve my back and poke my ass out behind the seat to keep my balance. That keeps the speed going as I pump my pedals on the flat and go right back down the last angle, get to the lip, ollie, and—fuck it!—I'm already leaning back hard as I pop off, feeling the world spin under me, toward me, and then away from me as I flip and land it.

Man, do I *land* it!

I hear people shout as I come down hard with my back tire first and I hear my chain kick up off the back cog and rattle through the spokes as I lose all my push underneath me. The pedals are useless now without a chain.

And as I hit the hand brakes and come to a stop in front of Kurtis and Little Nate and Akil, I see white faces around them. College kids maybe. Drunk certainly. And where they came from, I'll never know, but I know they're screaming in my face, they're so excited. I can smell the beer as words come at me in a crush: *awesome, raw, crazy, dude, unreal, sickest, amazing.*

All that stops when a siren starts and blue and red lights jump up only fifty feet from us. A black and white squad car cruises up the backside of Light and around, onto Pratt, trying to get closer to us.

Damn, I think. *Damn, damn, damn.*

The light sways away from me and goes out as Little Nate jumps on the back of Kurtis's bike. I'm blinking bright blue spots away from my vision but I can see the camera's still pointed at me as Kurtis gasses it a little to tell me to hurry, to tell me that he's waiting but he won't be waiting long.

So now I'm just dropping my BMX and running to my bike and starting it.

I'm looking for Akil but he's already out ahead of Kurtis, getting on Pratt. I'm getting on and following Kurtis.

I'm getting the hell out.

29

PUSHING IT

I don't even know what street I turn on, but I follow Akil. Buildings whip past me before we go hard left on a big street. Fayette, I think. It's past 1:00 in the morning and it's a good thing there's no cars out too. A delivery van here. A taxi there. But the rest of this city's got their eyes closed. At sixty miles an hour, things blur pretty good as you're going by them. You gotta make fast choices.

So the first thing I do is speed up.

I'm up beside Kurtis when I yell against the wind. "Why the hell are you shooting this?"

"Motherfucker, I'm saving your life," Little Nate shouts back at me. "Cops won't do nothing so long as we got a camera going. They know they're getting *witnessed*."

It hits me then that this is what Kurtis wanted. He wants us to push limits, move boundaries, to show the cops we can go anywhere we want when we put our minds to it.

It's safe up on Druid Hill—well, not safe, but *safer*. Safer from cops anyway. Downtown, you can't do exactly what you want. Kurtis wants a chase, wants attention, because it's the best way to top something. Little Nate back there filming, it's not by accident. I smash a right when Akil goes right. I get so low my knee almost touches the pavement and it makes my stomach sick.

If I'd touched, that would've been the end of me. I need to concentrate. I need to—

It hits me then. Maybe a little late, but it hits me.

This is the new video, I think. *Right here.*

It's sick and smart at the same time. And I know how Kurtis has that side to his nature where he just needs to push things. He doesn't know any other way. It's how he came up. How he became Kurtis in the first place. Pushing it is just who he is. It's his reason for living, to move the limit a little further away.

It wasn't really about the fountain and the flip. It was about the chase. And man is he getting one.

The cop's on me, agitating. Revving his engine hard to keep up.

Akil drops back to try to hound him off, but the car's not having it. It's stuck on me good.

Cops aren't supposed to chase, I think.

But they are and they're getting too close. Trying to bump my back wheel, trying to make me fall.

They're so close I can see the face of the driver and I don't expect to recognize it, but I do. It's Leonard. Looking exactly like he did outside City, passing out pamphlets. He smiles at me, but then he looks away, looks up the street to Kurtis and Little Nate and he falls back a little.

When he does that, I figure it's time to pay Akil back for saving my ass and Kurtis's the other night. I don't have hardly enough practice, but I'm still able to wheelie up at about forty miles and hour and gas it to fifty before slamming back down but keeping my bike under me with just a little wiggle.

Next I go up on the sidewalk and dare Leonard to follow me as I cut a corner. In my head, I'm thinking Akil and Kurtis can use this to get away.

I'm thinking they have to.

But it doesn't work.

I go left. Kurtis goes straight. Akil goes right.

Leonard goes right too.

Sirens are directional. You can tell when they're not following you anymore because it's not as loud.

I U-turn myself as quick as I can, having to slow down to about twenty or so to do it safely in one fluid motion and I get back going the other way. I see Leonard up ahead of me. Beyond that cop car, I see Akil, and as I'm shooting through an intersection I see Kurtis coming back around too, but he's slower than me.

I'm pouring it on to catch up, praying for some straight line speed as I see Akil go right at a red light, and Leonard's right behind him, and then me, and even from a hundred feet away I hear the car slam on its brakes, locking them up as it lays down rubber.

When I hit the corner and go right, I have to swerve to avoid the stopped cop car and beyond it, a delivery truck wide as hell and snugged up to the curb. Next to it is a figure, short, in a black hoodie. He's holding something up in his hand. A phone? A camera?

It must be, because there's light pouring out of it. White light from a flash, but continuous.

I let off the gas when I see Akil's bike on its side in the middle of the road.

It's twisted up and leaking fuel.

And right then everything inside me twists itself up too.

Because I know what I'm about to see before I see it, but when I do, it doesn't make it any easier. It makes it worse.

Ahead of me, about twenty feet, is Akil, face down in the street.

And he's leaking too. All around him is a big red puddle getting bigger. I've only seen blood once like that before.

And I can't go closer, so that's where I stop.

I know right away but I don't want to believe it.

He was dead the moment he hit.

I know because I know.

Seeing him lying there, I can only think on my momma and her red soles sticking out. How two big arms from a person I couldn't see held me tight from behind so I wouldn't go rushing into that house. It wasn't anything for a kid to see, they said. At the time, I was spitting mad, but now, seeing this, I get it.

Nobody needs to see this. Nobody.

I know I'll see it in my dreams forever.

The worst is Akil doesn't even have his shoes. He hit so hard they must've popped off. I look to the curb. I look across the street but I don't see them. Where they went, I don't even know.

It's just socks on his feet. A black one and a white one. The white's twisted back the wrong way and it's loose somehow.

And for a second I think how it's the saddest thing in the world how he didn't have socks that matched.

But that doesn't matter anymore.

I'm just sitting there, feeling dry like there's no liquid in me when I catch movement out the corner of my eye.

Leonard's off his radio and he's walking at me with his hands up, saying how he didn't mean to do it, how he couldn't have known about the delivery truck double-parked when he turned the corner.

But he doesn't look shaken up. He's got dead eyes. I don't believe a thing about him. He's not sorry. He's glad he did it. And then he's swiveling his head like he's looking around Little Nate's camera and maybe he's about to take a run at me, but he sees the kid in the hoodie with the phone up and flash on and decides not to.

"I saw what you did," the kid in the hoodie sounds like a little boy but I can't tell with the light in my face. "I saw you speed up and hit him!"

Leonard rocks back on his heels then and shakes his head, but I can just tell he's thinking about how to respond, so I take one look at his face and sneer with every last bit of hate I been hiding away inside me—hate that's just been building inside me my whole life and only now is it breaking off in chunks and floating up to the surface.

"You're gonna regret this shit," I say to him. "You just birthed another level."

He stands there, lights going blue and red through his big dumbo ears, going red and blue on the back of his shiny neck, and he opens his mouth but he's got no words.

I key in, gas my bike, and blaze.

The wind hits my sweat and turns me cold as I stare at Leonard standing behind me with his hands out, like I need to forgive him or something. I see him getting small in my side mirror I got. He disappears when I turn the corner and shoot off into the night.

I hope never works for him, because that's when I'll forgive what he did.

Never.

30

EVERYBODY GOT TO CRY SOMETIME

In the funeral home not much bigger than my aunt's living room, I find out that Akil's dad has the same forehead, nose, and chin as Akil, but not the same eyes.

Those are brown with a purple ring, filled up with disrespect.

The mouth's different too. It's ugly. Twisted up.

Kurtis is standing behind me, flowers hanging down in his hand because he hasn't had a chance to put them up yet. His face looks bad. All pale and thin. Not like he's been crying but like he might puke at any time.

But he sure puffs his chest up when Akil's dad looks right at me and says something about how it's probably my fault his son's dead and how I shouldn't even be here and I just step to him and stand in front of him, not going away, just staring him straight in his stupid face—this guy that couldn't even be bothered to be a dad to his own son and now he cares all of a sudden—and I look back and forth from him to the picture of Akil over the coffin: him standing in front of the row home with his mother when she wasn't too sick yet.

Just the two of them. No dad to be seen. That says it all.

I got posed in plenty like that growing up, except in Colorado Springs. They're standing in the Baltimore sun, though.

It must be summer in that picture.

I don't care about anything in this perfume-smelling place except that picture. I want to take it home with me and hang it up. Give it a place of honor.

I feel my aunt's hands on my arm, trying to pull me away. "I want that picture," I say.

Akil's dad looks to it. He says, "Never in a million years."

"That's cool," I say, and my voice sounds like me and not me—a cold I've never been before now. "I'm taking it anyway."

I shake off Aunt Blue as Akil's dad moves like he's about to stop me from running off with it, and Kurtis moves to step between us, but I just pull my phone out of my pocket.

And I put the frame in my frame.

And I click.

Aunt Blue said this phone is for emergencies only.

This is an emergency.

I can't not see Akil anymore.

He knew how it felt to be me.

Everybody's deflating after I put my phone in my pocket.

Kurtis walks off shaking his head. My aunt doesn't try to grab me again. Akil's dad fades back, sitting down woozy, almost like I punched him.

Grief is a weird thing. It's part time-travel device. Sometimes, you can be looking at something, swearing it's only for a second and then you look up and it's an hour later. Grief steals time. This, I know. And you never get it back like how you never get the person back.

It's just gone.

Later—I don't know how much later—when we're sitting next to each other in uncomfortable folding chairs and I'm squeezing an imprint of my momma's Valkyrie key chain into the palm of my hand, my Aunt Blue says to me, "You had a cousin."

I'm not sure why she's telling me this now. I don't know where Kurtis went either. Or Little Nate. Or anybody that was here before.

Maybe she thinks it'll help me.

"Noreen, her name was. Lived to four with CF and then her body just gave up." We both stare at the wall for a moment.

But it isn't.

It's longer than that.

"Aunt Blue," I hear myself say, "what's CF?"

"Cystic fibrosis," she says.

Later, she says, "Her dying like that is why I became a nurse. I never did get over it. Still haven't. Never will."

My aunt blinks those words away, almost like she's surprised she's said them.

But she doesn't regret telling me. I can tell. Even now.

Later, an old woman with skin like chewed-up gum comes by and tells us it's time to go. There's another funeral now.

See, grief's a time machine.

"Everybody got to cry sometime. I suppose it's somebody else's turn now." Aunt Blue says it like she knows what crying is all about. "Grey?"

But I'm turning away. "Grey?"

I'm walking.

Outside, it's raining down.

I look at a broken gutter until I hear Aunt Blue open up her umbrella next to me. Which wakes me up to the street.

Across from me I see the short dude from the night Akil died, standing like he's got something to say.

It's him all right.

Same height. Same black hoodie.

Not holding anything in his hand this time, though.

"Hey," I shout at him.

But he doesn't say anything back, he just takes off running, and I can't even begin to unravel why.

I take a step to go after him, but Aunt Blue's hand is on my arm again. I don't fight her.

I let her take me home.

31

SICK WITHOUT COUGHING

My aunt took my dirt bike away. She must have taken my keys after the funeral, but I didn't notice for three days because I was so behind on schoolwork. Aunt Blue even gave me a pass for not reading all of *Invisible Man*. She wasn't even mad at me, just told me to finish in the summer because school was more important right now.

Akil's death barely made the news. Two days before, a white girl from the University of Maryland got kidnapped—they *thought* she was kidnapped anyway. Her picture got put up on Fox 45, and she was blonde and blue-eyed and pretty if you're into that. Man, all of a sudden, *everybody* cared about her. Her crying mom got interviewed. It even went nationwide for a day, scrolling on tickers. Well, it turned out she wasn't even kidnapped. She had eloped with her corny-looking boyfriend to

Atlantic City—they didn't check in under their names because his parents wouldn't have approved. That's the world we live in, wild goose chases for white girls.

Akil dying only got a picture that looked like a mug shot on TV and a couple lines about how he was riding dangerously and if anybody had information to call P.O.S.S.E. and that was it. Nothing about Leonard or it being police-provoked. They said it almost like Akil deserved it.

I'm not saying all this because I'm mad about it (which I *am*), but because it's reality. If you're not on TV, you're invisible. If you don't put black people on TV, if you don't say what happens to us truthfully, we stay invisible.

Maybe YouTube is good because you don't have to wait around for people to show you, or your experience. You get to show it. That's the point.

News and reporters don't matter then. *You* matter.

It's like the antidote to the kind of TV where the darker you are, the less you matter. Because there's a message to that, right? Even if it's not said to your face, there's a message to it, and it's something like: stick to the shadows or go away.

Well, I don't want to stick to the shadows. And I don't want to go away. I'm not invisible. I'm doing my thing and dragging it out into the light. Every time I do a stunt, I want it documented. I need Little Nate for that, and I'm grateful to him even though I haven't said so yet. I want there to be something good left behind when I go.

I've been thinking about dying a lot lately. About not being here anymore.

My aunt says I've not been feeling well, and I guess she's right. It's like being sick without coughing. The problem with that, though, is you never know when you're getting better. Coughs can go away. Your body can recuperate. But some of these feelings are the same for me as when my mom died, and I don't know if they ever really left but are just coming back stronger.

Helplessness. Numbness. I got a lot of *ness*es rattling around in me. Probably more than I know yet, even if this all feels too familiar.

I got taken to the psychologist again the day after the funeral, but she said I didn't have to say anything, so we just stared at each other for an hour. It actually wasn't as bad as it sounds. I didn't mind being seen. And me not talking was probably for the best. If I would've talked, I would've said something that might have gotten me in trouble, something like, I don't necessarily want to die, but I don't care if I live.

People get upset if you say things like that. They write prescriptions. They put pills in you. They talk about suicide prevention, and they talk about wanting to talk more. I've already been down this road, though, and I don't need to do it all over again. It was bad enough the first time.

Besides, what these people don't seem to understand is that right now, I don't need to be talking. I need to be doing. That's therapy too. Actually doing something. And I've got a stunt in my brain.

It involves this little bit of the I-83 underneath the 41st Street Bridge that has a good-sized shoulder with concrete dividers on it. I'd need a ramp to get up on top of that. It's dangerous and crazy, especially because there's a drop on the other side. But that's what I need right now.

Something else to focus on. Something else to *do*.

So it's just as well that the doorbell rings and when I open it, it's Little Nate, checking up on me.

He leans back before he says, "You good?"

Right after he says it, he makes a face like he shouldn't have. He means am I good to go and hang out, not am I doing good, because we both know the answer to that. Words get weird like this when people die. Nobody wants to offend you or make you sadder than you are, but they can't help saying things they're already in the habit of saying.

I grab my coat and close the door behind me. I lock the deadbolt with my key. "Yeah," I say, "let's go."

I'm not good, though. Not even a little bit. I'm busted up inside, but I got to keep moving forward.

It's the only way not to fall apart.

32

THE WORLD KNOWS ABOUT YOU

When Little Nate and I get to Kurtis's place, there's people over, clogging up the living room, and it looks like they have been over for days because there's fast food containers stacked on tables and on top of the TV like little towers of Styrofoam and the trash can's overflowing with wadded-up napkins and plastic forks.

I don't say *what's up* to anybody because I'm dashing to the upstairs toilet because downstairs is taken. I should've gone before I left and I think everything's good when the door is somewhat ajar, so I push it open with a fist and I'm about to shut it behind me and lock it when I see Kurtis on his knees on the floor and I freeze.

He's doubled over the toilet, spitting into it. Beneath his chin, the water is a watery green. He's been puking. A lot. That's when the smell hits me and I cover my nose up as he swings his head toward me. He's got a scowl on his face and hate in his eyes. Hate that he's embarrassed. Hate that I saw him like this.

"Yo," Kurtis says, "get the fuck out!"

I've never seen him like this. Fragile. Sick. *Human*. It's scary, if you want the truth.

I say, "You okay?" But it's reflex. I knew I shouldn't have said anything.

Because his look coming right back at me says, no, he isn't okay, but didn't he just tell me to get the fuck out, and why am I not doing it?

So I do. I shut the door and go back downstairs to the other bathroom, which is open. When I'm done doing my thing, I roll out slow to find Kurtis is back downstairs.

I nod my hello at him. He's shirtless and sitting on the couch between two people I've never seen before. He's got a plate in his lap and he's drinking a glass of water.

"Drank too much last night," he says without looking at me, but his words aren't for anyone else.

It sounds more like an excuse than an explanation.

Monika looks up from the computer sitting on the little end table in front of the couch and smiles. I nod back.

She says to me, "You hungry?"

"No, thanks," I say. I don't tell her I haven't eaten much since Akil died, and only when Aunt Blue makes me.

She nods a suit-yourself nod and goes back to what she's looking at.

There's not really any place to sit in the living room, so I just stand and cross my arms, which is basically what I'm doing when Darryl and one of the guys who was with him that night come out of the kitchen with a sandwich. Darryl apologizes to me for the other day. It doesn't seem the sincerest thing in the world, and I know Mon put him up to it. He also introduces the other dude to me. His name is Michael, but he goes by Mike.

I'm about to introduce myself back, but Mike says, "Sorry to hear about your boy too. He sure could ride."

"Thanks," I say, but I'm not really sure what I'm thanking him for, apart from saying something nice about Akil.

Them being here means Darryl didn't get replaced, or they got called in, or I don't really know how it works and I'm not trying to put myself in the middle of it. It's Kurtis's call. His crew is his crew. All that matters to me now is that I'm still in.

"Hey, Air." Little Nate waves me over to the computer. "Did you see how the Safety City video hit its max?"

Air's my name now. Nobody calls me Grey anymore. Not here. I say, "I don't know anything about video caps," because I don't.

Little Nate explains that there's a limit to prevent artificially inflated numbers for the first twenty-four hours, and Safety City has maxed it out. He goes on to say this max just affects the number of views that appear on the page, and it doesn't reflect how many people actually watch it the first day. I'm listening but I'm not.

I'm thinking about Akil, about how good that day was in Safety City.

"On top of that," he says, "the night video did the same thing *and* it has over three thousand thumbs-up, more than twice the Safety City video, against only fifty-eight down *and* it has six hundred comments. Here, look."

Little Nate nods at Mon and she turns the computer to face me. I look at the video page and scroll down to the comments. Scanning through them, I see that most are encouraging and positive about what we're doing, but some aren't. A few call us thugs. A couple do worse than that. They're straight-up racist. That jars me a little.

I say, "Some people sure are free with that *n* word on here, huh?"

"They can be," Kurtis says.

It doesn't seem like it even fazes him anymore. He's been doing this for so long, but for me, it's new. It gets at me a little. I wonder what kind of homes these people come from that they think it's okay to say these kinds of things in public. I mean, sure, it's Internet-public, but it's still public.

The only good news about the comments is no one attacks my skill. They can see my face and think it looks stupid or ugly (a few say that), or they can call me *halfie* (like someone did) and that's fine, water off a duck's back, but if they try to fade me for what I did, that's different. And there's no shade here for my skill. Some people don't like the name Air, saying it's unoriginal (screw them), but nobody says I can't ride.

Not a single one. That means something to me.

"Sure looks like you two got a platform. The world knows about you." Little Nate turns to me then. "So what do you wanna do now?"

I look at Kurtis. Kurtis looks at me, and for a moment, it seems like everything is normal between us again.

"Hey," he says, "I got something for you."

"What?"

Kurtis shrugs and nods across the room where Darryl's already grabbing a big cardboard box up off the floor. He drops it in front of Kurtis without even grumbling or anything. He seems happy to do it.

When Kurtis opens the box, he pulls out a black T-shirt with white lettering on it that says I AM AKIL WILLIAMS.

I need to take a breath when I see that.

I mean, the T-shirt is nothing special. It's simple, really. But it makes my eyes hot. It makes me want to wear one.

And it feels right then like I've been set up, but set up in a good way, like they knew I'd want this. I'm cool with falling for it too, because I'm all the way in.

I wriggle out of the shirt I got on and into a brand-new large from the box. Kurtis does the same. After that, everybody does. Darryl. Mike. Monika. The other people.

Even Little Nate manages to get himself into an XXL.

"If we're about biking and only biking, we're never gonna get any bigger," Kurtis says, and I'm right there with him.

I say, "But if we're *about* something. Something bigger than us. Something even Akil would be proud of, well, then . . ."

I can't finish my sentence, but it doesn't look like I need to. All around me, people are nodding.

"One more thing," Kurtis says. He nods at Mike and Mike brings a box out from the kitchen.

When he opens it up, I freeze. I see Akil staring back at me.

Plastic masks of Akil's face, like the kind painted on thin white plastic for Halloween, sit stacked inside.

I don't know how he got them or where, but I know why. To make sure Akil didn't die for nothing. It's creepy in the right way, like, if we wear these and front the cops, we'll be reminding them every minute about what they did.

I shiver then, and I know I need to be outside and wearing it. I need to be riding.

I need to be doing Akil proud.

33

FREEWAY

Me just mentioning being out on the streets whips up a frenzy and throws us all out into the night. That's when I realized we all need to be out, need to be thinking about something else. If we sit, we think about Akil, and then nobody says anything, and nobody feels better. We all just spiral down and feel worse. So this ride—out in the night, out in the air—it needs to happen.

It *has* to. Or we'll all go crazy.

We're a few exits away from the 41st Street Bridge, on the shoulder of I-83, trying to set up a ramp so I can ride one of Kurtis's I-don't-care-if-you-crash-it dirt bikes up it and onto the concrete divider. After I get up on it, I don't know what I'll do.

Maybe I'll pull back on the handlebars and wheelie on my back wheel if it feels stable enough. I don't know. I'll have to play it by ear and figure it out when I get up there. I'm still wearing my mask too.

More people than you think are out at 2 a.m. on a Thursday morning. The interstate is empty, but not like *empty*-empty. There's at least a car a minute going by. That makes everybody nervous while me and Mike drag one of Kurtis's ramps out of the van and set it against the curve of the divider. Darryl would help too, but he had to go to work. Night shift.

"What about knockos?" Little Nate wants to know. "How much time we have?"

Mike corrects him. "Interstates aren't knockos, they're state police."

"It's whoever comes first," Kurtis says. "If a patrol stumbles onto you, they stumble onto you, but I been hearing they got P.O.S.S.E. detailed out west. Any calls come in about bikers being bikers, don't be surprised if it's routed straight there."

"I don't care which one it is," I say. "Leonard and Cogland can come shoot me if they want to, but I'm doing this."

"Damn," Little Nate says, "that's dedication right there."

I don't know if it's dedication, but it's something.

Kurtis's homemade ramps are okay, but not great. If I was smart, I'd just be down here with measuring tape, then go home and figure out how to build it, and come back later, but later isn't an option right now.

"This is your show," Kurtis says before I map out the plan. "For Akil."

I think about walking in on Kurtis in that bathroom being

ill, and maybe how he's not even okay enough to do this ride, but I still nod at the fact that he's giving me the spotlight. I'm grateful.

The key for all this is I need to be able to go up two and a half feet, but not at so steep a grade that I can't turn 90 degrees when I get to the top of a concrete divider, because if I can't do that, there's no way in hell I'm staying up. The other problem is, the divider narrows as it gets to its flat top. The width of it is probably three and a half inches, give or take, which is about the width of my tire. It goes about fifty yards and then exits on a much sturdier ramp. That just means no room for error. None.

Feeling the traffic going by, feeling them slow as they get close to us, just to see what we're doing, has got my heart going, though. And the best part is, they see my shirt when they see me. They see my mask.

I decide to do a test right away, so Little Nate does his thing and gets the camera rolling and keeps it rolling.

I try it once and lose balance as I'm going up the ramp and have to bail. The good news is I get far enough away from the bike that it doesn't land on me. The bad news is I land on my left forearm pretty good and then my whole body falls on top of it.

That takes my wind out.

When I get up, Mike says, "Bruh, you're bleeding."

I look at my arm. He's right. I've got a gash a few inches from my elbow, but it's not spurting. It's burning hot from getting ripped open on the asphalt, but it'll be fine. I've had worse. Me and pain, we know each other.

"Like nobody's ever bled to do this," I say.

For safety's sake, I turn the mask around on my head, so Akil is looking out behind me, watching my back so I can have full vision of what I'm about to do.

For his part, Kurtis just nods. He knows where I'm at.

I get the bike up and it's scuffed a bit from falling on its side, but it's good to run, so I go again.

This time I get up the ramp and get turned onto the top of the divider, but it's too tight an angle and I don't have enough speed, so I wobble off—back onto the shoulder—but this time when I bail, I land on my feet as the bike tips and comes down on its handlebars with a big damn crash.

Everybody winces when it hits, me most of all.

34

GO AGAIN

I'm back on the bike and checking it. One of the hand brakes, the left one, is almost hanging off the bar, but other than that, it seems fine, and it starts okay, so I go again. This time, Little Nate is behind me. He wants to show how thin the divider is, so he sets his camera on it, about fifteen feet back from the ramp.

My arm is numbing up on me, but I go again. I get up with the right speed, get turned, get my wheel locked in on the divider, and I'm going. I'm like a train on one rail.

This sparks a small celebration behind me.

Somebody screams, "oh, what!" but I don't know who. Kurtis maybe.

My center of balance is off a little bit because there's a space in between the two concrete dividers, because it isn't just one, it's two put back-to-back, not like a solid piece of concrete, and as a result, the middle bit is grabby. My tires are pumped up nice and high but it still affects me. I decide there's no way in hell I'm doing a wheelie on this.

There's no way.

When I'm going, fifty yards feels like 350, and I'm careful to slow down and exit out, but it works, and best of all, the ramp doesn't come out from under me as I'm going down it.

When I look back, everybody's cheering and laughing.

There's nothing like this feeling, knowing you're responsible for awe. I get how Kurtis can't stop doing it now. He's an addict. Maybe I am too.

I roll back to my first ramp and take some pats on the back before I go one more time. On this run, though, Little Nate shoots from the middle of the highway, the center divider. He tweaks his flash in a way that it just kicks out continuous light like a spotlight. It's probably dangerous as all hell for drivers but it won't be on that long.

Little Nate has shots in his head. One is: The big circle of light doesn't move. I ride through it. Out of the dark and back into the dark. Another is: I ride into the light and then it follows me up the ramp, and then I ride out of it. He thinks about this stuff a lot. All I care about is if he makes it look cool in the end, which he always does.

I do both the shots he wants. With my mask on front this time, pulled down a bit so I can see the divider beneath me through the eyeholes. And because it feels all right when I'm going, I pop a wheelie on both rides. Three feet in the air.

Two-hundred pound motorbike underneath me. A recipe for death if there ever was one. But I pull it off. Twice.

For the second one, a car stopped on the highway to watch me to do it. The car got going when Little Nate turned his light off.

It was an odd moment, me getting down on the ramp, transitioning to the asphalt and feeling safe again, feeling solid, and this old white lady drives by in her luxury car and I see her give me a thumbs-up and a wink as she goes by.

That throws me, so I tell the guys when I get back to the van and they get to laughing and saying how maybe she really liked me and that I needed to go for older women more often. I shrug it off while we load the ramps into the car. I can tell that none of us really believe the cops didn't show up, but none of us want to mention it, for fear of jinxing it.

But after we send the van off, as we're about to head back and check the footage, Little Nate decides we need B-roll, us doing something on the highway. We're pushing our luck being out here this long and nobody coming, but Little Nate can't help it. He's greedy like that. He's got such great stuff in his head that he's just trying to make it come to life.

"Something cool," he says, which could mean anything.

Mike looks at Kurtis.

Kurtis looks at me. "You wanna blind ride?"

35

JUST BLACK

I've never heard of blind riding before, so Kurtis feels the need to explain it, and then make it even tougher.

"Basically, you put on a blindfold, and you *go*," Kurtis says, "but I got an idea to take it to the next level." He walks up next to my bike, and he puts his left hand on my right throttle. "No *hands*."

I get what he's thinking: I keep the bike steady and he rides beside me and keeps the speed up. It's a terrible idea. Every possible thing could go wrong. He doesn't throttle both bikes exactly the same way, he speeds up or I slow down and he loses hold of my handlebars or they get away from him, he'll need to shout quick for me to grab, and then somehow, I'd have to have it under control enough to slow down, pull my blindfold, and stop safely. You know what? It'd actually be safer for him to ride behind me on my own bike and work the gas and brakes, looking out from under my arm or something, but this—*this* is crazy.

"If you do this"—Kurtis says it like he's got something on his mind, almost like he could use this as a test or something—"you can do anything—even jump off a building."

For a second I think about how impossible that sounds, but only for a second. I know he's planting a seed, and I let him.

"Let's do it," I say.

Kurtis explodes into laughter right as a car goes by us, the red of its parking lights shooting off into the night. He laughs even harder when I take my shirt off and roll it up into a blindfold, making sure to position it so only the word *Akil* is showing.

That's the part I want over my mask and eyes. Almost like he can be my eyes now. Almost like he can guide me.

I get it positioned on my forehead. It's lumpy and long the way it droops behind me, but it ties and it holds. I don't pull it down over my mask yet. I'll wait to do that until we're going over forty miles an hour on the interstate. Little Nate's in front of us, sitting on the back of Mike's bike. He has twisted himself around in the seat and he's got the light on me. It's almost blinding.

When we're up and going, Kurtis is right up beside me, moving at exactly the same speed. Close enough to touch. He reaches over to my throttle and we do a few tests to make sure we can do simultaneous speed. It's Goldilocks stuff.

The first one is too loose on the throttle. The second one is too tight.

The third one is just right.

We nod at each other after that. We got this. Through the wind, he shouts, "Okay!"

I let go of my handlebars. My stomach does a flip inside me but after a few seconds it finally gets right-side up.

That's when I pull the blindfold down and the plastic of the mask mashes around my eyes and cheeks as I do.

Before that, I see the lines of the interstate flicking by me, I see the median flying by, I see Kurtis leaning in and balancing his bike perfectly, like some sort of circus performer—and then I don't.

It's just black.

My fingers make a scratching sound over the screen-printed letters covering my eyes, and it's not like I say a prayer or anything, but I do say to Akil that if he's out there somewhere, if he's watching this, I'd appreciate whatever protection he can give.

Kurtis keeps shouting at me through the wind. "Slight bend right," or "It's a flat straightaway. Reach out, man! Grab that night with two hands!"

I feel an unnatural rush of wind on my left and I'm sure it's Mike breaking so he can go behind us and have Little Nate film from there.

I'm cold, but I'm not.

It's the stupidest thing I've ever done in my life. I'm scared to death, and I love every second of it. It's not numbness. It's not any kind of *ness*.

And that's the best feeling of all, the way it wipes everything else out. It's fear, it's heart thumping, it's breathing too fast . . .

And I get what Kurtis said now, how if I can do this, I can do anything. Jumping while being able to see would be nothing compared to this.

Doesn't matter the height.

Because right now this is me spreading my arms out, trying to catch the whole night up in my hands, and rushing through blackness.

Which is exactly why I hear sirens before I see them.

36

PURSUIT

As I'm grabbing my handlebars back, I feel Kurtis let go. I push my blindfold back up on my forehead and have to use two hands to adjust my mask. Once I do, the whole road opens itself back up to me. I see two taillights way up ahead but nothing else. Behind me the blue-and-reds are going crazy and the siren's going nonstop.

I watch Kurtis as he grimaces and gives me a quick nod before ripping out in front of me. He's the fastest, and we need him to run point on this.

Behind me, Little Nate has that floodlight flash of his on the cops to give them some of their own medicine. How many people have they ever done that to? Of course they don't like it when someone does it to them. They shout something out over the speaker that the wind rips away from me.

Next to me on the road I see Mike's headlight sway back and forth as the cruiser comes close to him on the side, trying to scare him enough to lose control. It's the craziest thing I've ever seen because Little Nate is holding his camera up and screaming something at them as he kicks at the driver's side door of the cop car and dents it.

I don't know how Mike holds them up through that. I mean, I don't think I could even do that if somebody was trying to swipe me and Little Nate was throwing his weight around on the back of my bike. It takes strength and balance to hold steady. It's athletic as hell. Gives me a whole new appreciation for Mike and his skill.

And part of me wants to believe it's Mike's skill that's backing the cop car off, but I know it's Little Nate and his camera, him waving it in their faces.

We shoot under the 41st Street Bridge. I grab a quick look at the speedometer: sixty-five miles per hour, and I was going at least that blind. But that's our rule tonight, nothing over the limit. Can't be adding anything more to what we've already done.

Going south, the plan is to head straight to Druid Hill Park, so I do that. Only problem is, you have to ride past pretty much the whole park first because there's nowhere to exit. My headlamp catches nothing but trees swaying beside me for a good couple miles before my sign pops up and I'm so damn happy to see it: 28TH STREET, DRUID PARK LAKE DRIVE, ½ MILE.

The brown sign for the Baltimore Zoo is right after that. USE EXIT 7, it says.

For cops that aren't supposed to chase, they're sticking with us pretty strong.

I'm under one more bridge, onto the exit ramp, and I'm up into the park like butter getting spread on hot toast. I pass the pool where Akil and I rode that very first time, a place I haven't been since he passed. It hits me real fast with a good memory of finding my flow, and how much more simple things were then, and how it never even occurred to us that we could get hurt.

I've got to shake that off, though.

I've got to get my mind right and stay focused on the present.

The best thing about dirt bikes is we don't need roads. We can go where cars can't. Scattering twigs and loose pebbles as I go, I leave the asphalt on Swann and roll up over a hill, short-cutting to the zoo's parking lot (which is still half full with the cars of people doing night-shift maintenance and cleaning). As I'm rolling down the backside of the hill, I switch off and go dark. No more motor. No more lights.

I glide into the parking lot, right to where our van is parked (which is right where I'd suggested it to be), and the ramps are down too, so I slow as much as I can and roll in with one fluid motion, braking as I'm going up and stopping before I hit the back of the seats with my front tire.

Mike's right behind me, with him and Little Nate pushing the bike up the ramp. When they're both safely in, we shut the doors and everybody gets down, peeling eyes for the cruiser, which sure enough crests over the hill and stops to turn its little search light on the parking lot.

I'm flat on my back and looking up at the ceiling when I see the light cut through the windows and throw shadows all around the van.

The light sweeps through once, and then twice.

We can almost feel them getting frustrated. Up until now, they've never had to deal with this. It was always simple chase stuff. Not this, though. Now it's time to outsmart them and let them know it.

They're stupid for thinking we'd do what we did before, that we wouldn't plan.

Not planning got Akil killed, and I'll be carrying that with me the rest of my life.

We'll never be doing that again.

The light pops off and the cruiser comes closer to the lot before gunning it back up another hill. Right then we all know they're thinking we're still riding, just faster.

When we can't see their taillights anymore, everybody breathes a sigh of relief. "Hell yeah," Kurtis whispers from his spot slumped down in the shotgun seat. "Good going, y'all."

I say, "Who was that anyway? State police?"

Mike gives me a look like, *you're joking, right?* before Little Nate says, "Who do you *think* it was?"

"Leonard," I say, and just hearing the man's name pop out of my mouth brings up a whole mess of hate.

"Nah," Little Nate says. "It was Cogland. He got real close too. And I got it all on camera. I was just screaming out, 'Go on and try to kill me, motherfucker! Go on and try to get me like Akil, because I'll get it all on camera!' You *know* he backed off after that."

37

EXPAND THE BRAND

Little Nate's telling the story of how everything went down and nobody in the living room at Kurtis's place can really believe it worked as well as it did, that we had the time to pull off the filming, that Little Nate got all the shots he wanted, that Cogland came, and that we still fooled him on the getaway. Little Nate told everybody I came up with that plan and people almost applauded. It was crazy.

After that, Little Nate gets it into his head that he needs to reenact the stunt for everybody, especially Monika, using the table as the concrete divider, making dirt bike noises and everything. He's really into it, but she's not exactly paying attention because she's trying to check out my forearm, and right then Kurtis gives me the best compliment anybody ever got.

"I couldn't have done that," he says to me, and he means it.

I can see it in his eyes, the way they're sparking, but I also can't help thinking of him in that bathroom, and I wonder if there's more meaning to it. Like right now, maybe he really couldn't have pulled it off the way I did.

"Whatever," I say. "You could've done it."

"Not at the drop of a hat like that."

I'm going to say something to disagree with him but peroxide gets swabbed over my arm and I wince instead of responding.

"Sorry," Monika says, and shrugs her shoulders, like she's sorry it hurts, but it needs to be done, so it's getting done.

The rest of the room is back to talking about the chase. Questions fly back and forth, individual conversations pop up, and in the middle of it all, Kurtis holds court.

But I'm more interested in my arm right now. There's a jagged little cut near my elbow joint that looks like somebody stuck a nail in me and ripped. The pressure I've been putting on it since being in the van has stopped the blood a little, but with the dried blood wiped off, it's right back to seeping.

It seems rude not to acknowledge Monika as she's fixing me up, so I say, "Seems like you've got a lot of experience with this stuff."

She gives me a smile that I feel deep in my chest. Just seeing it reminds me that it's been a long time since a pretty girl smiled at me like that.

She says, "Whatever gave you that idea?"

I look at her to see if she's joking, but I can't tell. "Just that you're with Kurtis and he always—"

She cuts me off. "I was joking."

"Oh," I say, feeling stupid.

"I'm thinking about studying to be a nurse," she says.

"I thought you were doing paralegal stuff, though," I say, "and trying to be a lawyer someday?"

"That someday is pretty far away. Being a nurse is quicker. Working quicker. Making money."

I nod. It makes sense, but the way she says it, it sounds like there's something else pushing those words. I don't ask what, though. I just say, "I think you'd be a good one. A good nurse."

She gives me a look like I must not really mean what I said, that I'm just being nice. "What makes you say that?"

"My aunt's a nurse. The one I'm staying with. I think you've got the head for it. You're really calm."

"Thanks," she says as she grabs up some plastic thread and a needle. "With your aunt being a nurse and all, that means you won't freak out on me when I stitch, right?"

"I'll be all right," I say, "but that doesn't mean I have to look either."

"Deal," she says, and laughs before doing what she has to do.

Kurtis looks at us then, like he's not so much checking on how I'm doing, but why Monika's laughing with me like that. And I'm not sure what he's seeing, because on my end, it's just getting stitched up. He raises a bottle to me then, and turns away.

The last part of me getting fixed is her checking if there's more damage than just a cut, like a break maybe. I tell her I've had broken bones before and I'm pretty sure this isn't one, but she asks me if I can move my wrist 360 degrees and I say I can, but it's not enough, so she makes me show her. I get about to 270 and have to stop.

After that, she uses her thumb to lightly press on my arm near my wrist. "Does this hurt?"

I must make a face, because she says, "Okay, it might be a sprain, or you might have some ligament damage."

This isn't exactly music to my ears.

"I think you should get this checked out when you can."

"Okay," I say, and as I say it, I'm already thinking of ways to explain this to Aunt Blue and I'm not coming up with anything good.

"Looks like you're set then," she says. "You were a good patient."

I thank her for taking care of my arm, and when she moves off to the kitchen, she takes a few girls with her. Little Nate plops into her spot on the couch and almost catapults me right out of it. He doesn't even notice. He's too busy waving Mike and Kurtis over and starting up a small huddle with just us four.

"Now's as good a time as any to let you know about this," Little Nate says it just above a whisper, "but we need to expand the brand. The footage from tonight is gonna light it up, and we need to be able to *capitalize* on that. We need to build!"

I don't even know what that means exactly, and I'm about to say so, but I stop myself because Kurtis and Mike are nodding, so I don't say anything.

I figure I'll find out soon enough.

38

AIR RAILROAD

I sure find out what it means when I get asked to take a walk to the garage, though, because there's a flag hanging out there with a logo on it, which is weird because I don't think anybody expected to see that. It's a black train with wings on a white background. It looks pretty slick, I got to give it that, but I just don't know what it's for.

"We're bigger than Baltimore now," Little Nate says, "and this's a symbol for people to rally around. It says, we're here. We're no invisible men. If you feel the same way, join us."

When I hear *invisible men* said like that, I know I have to give Little Nate credit for listening way better than I ever thought he could. Kurtis and Mike are nodding at that, and not in a surprised way, but in a way that they're looking at my reaction. That's when I feel like everybody's been talking behind my back, like they've been cooking up something without me and now they're springing it.

"It's a movement," Little Nate goes on, "to be visible, to be free."

I say, "This movement already got a name?"

Little Nate's eyes flash, like he was hoping I'd ask that question.

"I was thinking," he says to everybody, but mostly to me, "Air Railroad." When I blink, he adds, "But, you know, I'm open to suggestions too."

"We didn't talk about that," Kurtis says, basically confirming what I figured: They've all been working on this, talking about it already.

Mike points at me. "Air Railroad, like Air's railroad?"

"No," Little Nate says, "Air Railroad like—"

Kurtis cuts him off. "Like the Underground Railroad? It wasn't an actual railroad either. It was a path to freedom out of darkness. And air like, we catch air—same as with bikes and parachutes, right?"

Little Nate's looking excited now. He's bouncing on his toes a little because he can see the spark he set becoming a fire.

"'A path to freedom out of darkness,'" he says. "I like that."

I jump in then and say, "You think that's such a good idea, though, bringing up the whole slavery thing with it?"

"I hear you on that, but it's not about slavery," Little Nate says. "The Underground Railroad was about being hidden for the sake of survival. These days, we need the exact opposite.

We've got to be *seen*, we've got to be on video and posted up, or they'll just wipe us out and act like it never happened."

That one hits the room hard and we all get quiet for a minute. We know how true that is.

Finally, Little Nate breaks the silence by saying, "I got a slogan and everything too." He grabs a notebook sitting by the flag and flips to some sketchy-looking letters on a white piece of paper. He holds it up so we all can see it.

It reads: *Only for Those Who Live to Be Free.* Mike's smiling and Kurtis is right there with him.

Personally, I don't mind it. It looks real cool. The letters have a movement to them. They look like they might just fly right off the page. At that point, it's obvious Little Nate has spent a lot of time with this. He's been game-planning it like crazy, right down to how he was going to tell me about it too, I'm sure.

I say, "Earlier you said we were bigger than Baltimore—"

"We're worldwide." Little Nate grins so deep after he says it that he gets little fat folds in his neck. "People from thirty-six countries have looked at, and commented on, our videos. I'm talking places like Japan, South Africa, England, and Russia. We're hitting crucial demographics hard, action sports, hip-hop culture, millennials, all that."

He explains he knows this because he reads the comments— all of them—and there's also a tracking system called *analytics* that allows him to see where people are watching the video from. Just the Safety City video by itself has over 5,000 comments and over 200,000 hits, and that was by this afternoon.

Two hundred *thousand*. It's basically going everywhere at the speed of light.

"Now just imagine, if only half of those people gave you a buck," Little Nate says, "that'd be a hundred thousand dollars. What would you think about that?"

Those words suck the oxygen out of the room. They make everything about this conversation so much more real. For a few seconds, nobody says anything. We just stare at each other.

It's Kurtis that says, "So what do we have to do?"

Little Nate smiles like he's glad he finally got asked. "I'll put a website together with all the videos. Maybe I'll put up some smooth still photos. Other than that, I'll put a tip button on there to process online payments, but maybe we don't call it tips. We'll call it a donation, like it's helping the good work, and then encourage people to give."

Since nobody asks why, I do. "Why would people pay us to do what we're already doing for free?"

"Because we're not getting paid being up on YouTube and the stuff you guys do is dangerous. People get that, and they want to see more of it. I think with this new video focusing on Akil's memory, that'll also show that you're not just here to amuse people. You're here to accomplish something. And that's what the money is for. It helps you do what you want. Money makes the impossible possible."

It's not that I disagree with any of what's being said. I guess I just worry that money—any money—will change things, especially when I'm not even sure what all this is without Akil.

"I'm not against it," I say. "I just want to make sure we do right by Akil, by his memory and everything."

Everybody's looking down and nodding, so maybe I'm hitting the right notes with what I'm saying here. I keep going. "And maybe there's even a way we could make sure we give back with whatever money comes in. Maybe we set up a foundation or something, like how athletes do."

I'm thinking of Carmelo Anthony and his center that Akil and I rode past the night we saved Kurtis after his jump. That's when I start wondering what an Akil Williams center could look like. Would it be like a big, empty dirt lot with hills on it? Would it be a place where kids could ride all kinds of bikes, and even learn to ride?

It's real easy to get lost in a dream like that.

Kurtis clears his throat. His eyes are on the garage door, but they're focused far beyond it. "More stunts, bigger stunts. Better cameras, more angles. I mean, why not? We're already coming at it like professionals."

He stops himself. Far off, there's sirens. Maybe on the other side of the park. He talks over them.

"We'll do another jump." Kurtis rubs his chin. "But with two people this time, not one. And bigger. The Transamerica Tower. Tallest building in Maryland."

I scoff and look to Little Nate like Kurtis can't be serious. I look to Mike.

Neither looks surprised. And that's when I feel like I walked right into a trap. This is what the blind ride was all about:

getting me ready to say yes to something crazy.

And this right here is the something crazy.

"Doing that stunt shows how we can do anything," Little Nate says with his eyes down on the floor. "We won't be pushed back into the void like so many other young black men."

I mean, sure, that sounds good, but Little Nate isn't jumping! Brave words don't count when the person saying them isn't putting his ass on the line.

It's going to be on Kurtis and *on me*. That much is clear right about now. And I've never jumped anything but a bike.

When I finally say something, it sounds like my aunt's words coming out of my mouth. "What? Two jumpers just to be crazy, to be different somehow?"

"No," Kurtis says, and his eyes are sparking, looking livelier than I've seen them since Akil passed. "Two jumpers means we survive. It's strategy. Misdirection. Cops won't expect two. At least one will get away, and if that happens, Air Railroad keeps going. For Akil. And only for those who live to be free."

39

DIFFERENT TYPES OF FREEDOM

I'm in the kitchen, having lunch with Aunt Blue, when the phone rings. Somehow, without even picking up, I just know it's Little Nate. I haven't heard from him since our talk in the garage a couple days ago. We've been laying low because P.O.S.S.E. are out in force. Patrolling all hours. Really cracking down on riders. A lot of that is because of us, for what we've been doing. But the worst thing happened last weekend during a Sunday ride on the other side of the Hill, when a dude that was new at riding crashed into a little boy and smashed his teeth right out of his mouth. We couldn't even believe that when we heard.

"Miss Monroe's residence," I say into the phone, just like how Aunt Blue taught me to.

She blinks at me from the table, like, *is it for me?*

I shake my head at her right as Little Nate launches in without even saying hey. "The freeway video broke out," he says. "Most hits ever. It's all kinds of viral in Japan and Korea. Man, they *love* what we're doing over in Asia! Numbers don't lie."

I step into the hall on the other side of the kitchen for a little bit of privacy. I know Aunt Blue isn't too fond of that, but she doesn't say anything.

I say, "How many hits?"

"Got past three hundred thousand yesterday," Little Nate says.

"Damn," I say, but I draw it out in a long whisper.

"Grey Monroe!" Aunt Blue calls me out on it from the kitchen. *Damn* is short for *goddamn* in her book, and she doesn't abide that in her house.

I cover the receiver and say to her, "I'm sorry, ma'am."

"That's better," she says.

I uncover the mouthpiece and say back to Little Nate, "Why do you think this one is hitting harder?"

"I don't know," Little Nate says, but I know he knows, or at least he's been thinking about it a lot, because that's what he is—a thinker. "It's not just the stunts people are connecting with now."

I don't even need to ask what the other thing is. I know he'll spill it if I just keep listening.

"It's the message too, but it's both, you know? Can't have one without the other. All message? You bore people. All action? That's not enough content. It's got to be both. It's got to be *in harmony*. Because a stunt is just a stunt, right? It could be anything and it's gone in a moment, but when you got something to say, it's not a stunt anymore." He pauses there like he's waiting for me to take it in. "It's an *expression* of what you believe."

After that, he drops the heaviest thing on me: We've gotten $66,015.38 in donations so far, and it's growing.

That number makes my ears ring like I got slapped. I say, "*How* much?"

But my voice sounds far away to me, like it's in the next room and not coming out of my mouth.

"I'm watching it go up right now," he says, and I hear his finger *click-click*ing on his mouse. "Damn, somebody just gave us two hundred bucks. Just like that. One click. Money in our pockets."

We don't talk much after that. I'm in shock and he's told me what he needs to tell me, so we say bye and I hang up.

I go back over to the table and I sit in front of Aunt Blue and it's probably a bad idea, but I decide to tell her. Right then. About the hits, the money, everything. Well, almost everything.

When I tell her how many hits, she stops chewing a bite of her salad.

She puts her fork down when I tell her how much money has come in just a few days. She's quiet for a while after that. Outside, down the block, I hear dueling lawn mowers as a couple neighbors get to mowing their lawns. Aunt Blue has been different lately. Depressed, maybe. I think she thinks she's losing me, and I know for her that's extra bad, because she's already lost one kid.

"Could do a lot of good in Baltimore with that money. Could help a lot of people," she finally says, and shakes her head, which seems to wake her up a little. "Air *Railroad* though? Like, flying trains?"

"Like flying to freedom," I say. "Breaking shackles of gravity, of what people think young black men are in this country—"

She waves her hand at me to stop. "Okay, but what kind of freedom is it?"

I don't get what she's asking, so I say, "What do you mean what kind?"

"Oh, honey, there are different types of freedom and you just don't know it yet. Freedom from not being in jail. Freedom to express who you are and what you do. Freedom to determine your own destiny. But how free are you if people are paying—" She stops what she's saying right there when she sees me open my mouth to disagree with the word. "— oh, sorry, *donating* to you to do a certain thing? That means they'll want a whole lot more of it, and you'll have to keep giving it to them, but more next time. You'll have to top it and top it, until you can't top it anymore and they get bored and go somewhere else. And what's the cost of all that to you? I'm not talking in dollars. I'm talking spiritual cost. If you can't grow, if you can't fulfill your potential and who you're supposed to be."

In the quiet of her driving in her point, I can tell one of the mowers has stopped up the block. Now it's just one.

Aunt Blue picks back up. "So maybe you have to ask

yourself, is what's freeing me in the short run, locking me down in the long? Is it making people have unfair expectations of me? Is it limiting me? Or is it forcing me to be something I'm not?"

I've never thought of it that way before. Not any of it.

Aunt Blue can tell too. She knows she won on this, but nothing about her seems like she's rejoicing in it. She just seems exhausted as she gets up from the table and slides into the living room, *skish-skish*ing in her slippers until she's on the carpet and then just padding off to her room.

When she comes back, she's got a book in her hands.

"Maybe you'll get through this one," she says with some sass in it.

And that's funny, because it's a kid's book, super thin, with picture pages.

Henry's Freedom Box, it's called.

"Maybe it's all right being in a box for a while," she says, "but at some point, you have to get out, which means that when you do, you better make sure that you're exactly where you want to be."

She pushes the book at me across the table, sits back, and crosses her arms.

That's when I know for sure I can never tell her that when Kurtis and Little Nate and Mike were staring at me like I was their only hope in the world of making that jump off the Transamerica with two people and making sure everybody was talking about Air Railroad and remembering the name of Akil

Williams that I said yes after they promised I'd get some sky-diving practice in first.

Nothing would make Aunt Blue understand why I said yes, or even try to understand.

She'd just kill me before the ground ever had a chance to.

40

PUBLIC ENEMIES

I'm at Kurtis's the next day after school and Monika's in the kitchen baking up some chicken. Kurtis is sitting on the opposite end of the couch from me, reading a book with one eye because he says he's got a headache. Aunt Blue knows I'm here. She's going to pick me up when her day shift's done. I think she's a little more open to me doing all this with the money being involved, even though she won't say it. She still keeps talking about greater responsibility and greater good and challenging me to be better, both for myself and for Akil.

It's what I need to hear, even if it's not always easy to hear.

I'm doing geometry homework, and I'm actually kind of digging it because we're doing triangles right now, determining angles and figuring out surface area and stuff like that. The formulas are actually fun for me because I don't think of the triangles as some obscure shapes on pieces of paper, but as *ramps*, and in my head I'm grading every one on how difficult it would be to get up, and how far I could launch off it. That definitely makes homework better.

So I'm working on determining the angles of a particularly weird-looking scalene and grading it in my head as a bad ramp (because it's too steep), when a key rattles in the lock and Little Nate rushes in and slams the door behind him.

He's sweating like I've never seen him sweat before. It's just running off him like he walked in out of the rain. He must've dashed all six blocks from his house to here.

"Damn," Kurtis says to him, "where's the fire?"

Little Nate's almost breathless. "We got to push the plan up. Not in a month. Sooner. A *lot* sooner."

Kurtis scoffs and says, "Why?"

Little Nate doesn't say anything. He just picks up the remote and turns the TV to Fox 45. The screen pops on and shows a press conference halfway through and the worst part about it is that I recognize the person in the middle of it. But something's off. On the screen in a little graphic under his face. It says, SERGEANT COGLAND.

I say, "Why does that say *sergeant* next to his name?"

"Promoted," Little Nate says, still gulping for breath.

I got no words for that so I just bite my lip.

Monika comes in with a plate full of chicken right then too. Enough for everybody. But nobody makes a move for it. It just sits there steaming on the coffee table as we're all frozen, staring at the TV.

It gets worse.

After Cogland gives some quick BS about Akil's death, calling it *an unfortunate incident*, before saying how an investigation is ongoing into the behavior of the officers at the scene. That makes me want to punch someone. I can still see Leonard's face in my mind. It'll be there forever.

Cogland goes on and on about the dangers of irresponsible kids like us riding bikes on city streets, putting average, everyday ordinary citizens in peril (that's actually the words he used) and he name-checks that boy that got hit and says how it's P.O.S.S.E.'s job that such a thing never happen again. Ever. In order to do that, he says it's time to take some players off the streets.

A photograph comes up on the screen then and it's Kurtis. In case we didn't know, though, it says ALIAS: KURTIS underneath.

My mouth goes bone-dry.

It's a still from one of the earlier videos that Little Nate did a few years ago, and Kurtis is smiling in it. When they formed P.O.S.S.E. in the first place, he said we'd end up being the bad guys, and here it is. Now it's true.

"Ha," Kurtis says then, "*told* you! I hate it when I'm right."

The words used to describe him are *Public Enemy*, but he's not the only one.

Another fuzzy still-frame goes up on the screen next.

This time it's my face. From the Safety City video. Soon as I see it, my stomach drops right out from under me, like a bomb out some bomb bay doors in a WWII movie. And the worst part is, it says ALIAS: AIR underneath it.

This is more serious than serious.

"Oh, *shit*," I say, and all I can think about is how Aunt Blue is going to lose it when she finds out, and she will find out—I just hope I'm the one to tell her and not somebody else. For a stone-cold second I wonder if she will turn me in herself.

"Not bad," Little Nate says then, "but they could've pulled a better one from the Safety City video."

I just stare at him for that. At a time like this, of all the things to say, he's critiquing the photo choice.

The press conference ends quickly after that, and it cuts to a pretty black newscaster with natural hair who says, "P.O.S.S.E. urges anyone with information on these two individuals to contact B.P.D. immediately."

Nobody in the room moves, not even a muscle. Except me. I'm shaking a little. Chicken keeps steaming where Monika set it.

I can't focus on anything after that—definitely not on geometry homework—and the worst part about it is Kurtis is fine with it real quick. Little Nate is too. And they're trying to get me to be fine with it.

"Sooner or later we were all gonna have to be outlaws," Monika says, "and maybe we always were. They're just finally noticing."

Nobody questions Monika's use of *we*. She's with us, even if she doesn't ride. "They must be getting desperate too," Little Nate says. "You don't put stuff like that up on TV if you've got all kinds of leads and ways to arrest people. Besides, we don't need to worry about it just yet. Nobody comes forward in B-more unless there's money in it."

"True," Kurtis says. "If they put a bounty on us, it'll get real rough. But for now, we just got to get smarter and start thinking about how we can use this."

I can't really believe what I'm hearing, and it's not like I need to say so. They all can see I'm not buying into this.

"Air, this was always going to happen if we did it right, and maybe I didn't prepare you, and I'm sorry for that." Kurtis puts his hand on my shoulder. "But you can't get too big without people noticing. And besides, Cogland *is* the system. He's not gonna punish one of his own! When's the last time you heard of that happening? You watch, the same way I called us being villains before, I'm calling this: Leonard's gonna get away with it. Gonna get away clean too. Maybe even get promoted like Cogland. And let me ask you this, is that really a system you want to be supporting?"

That cuts my worry in half but doesn't kill it. What he's saying makes sense. And Kurtis can see it's hitting me. He lets go of my shoulder. He knows I just need to think about it. And I do, for an hour.

I go through a million scenarios in my head and I seem to end up in jail in every single one of them. The only thing that stops that thinking is Little Nate checking email on his laptop.

"Oh," he says as he hunches down to look at the screen, "hold up."

Kurtis says, "What?"

"We just got an email from *The New York Times*. They've been on the website. They've heard about P.O.S.S.E. and they want our side of the story."

After that, he just laughs, and right then Kurtis turns to me.

"Well," he says, "you didn't want to be invisible. Now we're not. Even better, somebody just handed us a bullhorn to say whatever we want. We can tell them about Akil, about what Leonard did. We can do *good*."

When he puts it that way, it seems like this will all be for something. Akil made his sacrifice, and now I have to do the same in order to make sure it wasn't for nothing. It's a weird feeling being scared and excited at the same time, worried about what's coming, but looking forward to it. I guess more than anything I just hope I can be good enough in explaining whatever we need to explain, that people will get it when we talk.

And the craziest thing about all this is, the *Times'* interview request isn't the last email from a news place that we get, and it's not the biggest.

Not by a lot.

41

DON'T GET IT TWISTED

Getting ready to do an interview is the scariest thing I've done in my life, especially since I'm already torn up about Akil and worrying what Little Nate said about pushing up the plans means for me. Like, does that mean I get less training time? The phrase "a bundle of nerves" has never made sense to me until now. Everything gets to me like I've got no armor. Lights. Sounds. Thoughts. *Everything*.

I've been worried about Cogland scooping me up ever since the P.O.S.S.E. announcement came out. That's why Aunt Blue said it was okay for me to take a sick day yesterday. I haven't even gone to school since it aired, but that doesn't mean Cogland can't go get my information from the school and show up. Aunt Blue already called them up and made it clear she didn't want her address shared with anybody. If the police wanted it, they needed a warrant or a court order. I don't know how much good that'd do, but it's something.

For what it's worth though, Mon said she never understood Cogland's angle, like what he was trying to accomplish by putting our faces up on TV? He said we were public enemies, but didn't say what crimes we committed. And they can't arrest us from video without a complaint and a witness. So maybe he was trying to get both from putting us out there, or maybe he just wanted to make us so visible that when people saw us they could report us before we ever really did anything. If he wanted to poison the community against us, it might've worked with older folks, but it made us heroes with people our own age, and since we already had a cause, they wanted to join.

Still, the fear of not knowing what comes next, of when this next jump is coming off and if I'll even be prepared, or of being caught and arrested at some point has been eating at my stomach ever since, and now I'm pacing the oil-stained floor of Aunt Blue's friend's garage.

I didn't even really want to do this interview, but Kurtis said I had to because I knew Akil the best, and I couldn't argue with that. He said I wanted to be visible and this is what it means now: I just have to step up. Because this isn't for a boring old newspaper. It's for TV.

National TV. And now our interview will get shown everywhere, Little Nate says. In airports. In Nebraska. In Alaska. In every other state too, even the ones that don't end in *ka*. And it will be the only interview we ever grant. Anything else we have to say we put on our channel and upload ourselves. Little Nate says doing it that way is the best path to keep it mysterious. He says you have to be exclusive.

The reason we're doing this in a garage is because the producer or the director—I don't remember which—wanted to show dirt bikes in the shot, so a garage was the only logical option. Little Nate hung the flag up behind us and everything, just like the first time I saw it at Kurtis's. He even checks the framing in the camera by looking in the eyepiece and doesn't care that the photographer guy gives him a funny look.

"Hey man," Little Nate says to the guy nonchalantly, "I've shot everything these guys have ever done, and I need to make sure it's representing us right."

There are lights everywhere, mostly big rectangular ones on tall stands. I can feel their brightness in my skull. They're all plugged into a surge protector by the workbench. Aunt Blue's standing next to that, trying to be out of the way, but trying to keep her eye on everything while still carrying on a conversation because that's just who she is. Monika's there next to her, chatting right back. They liked each other immediately, which was no surprise to me. Darryl and Mike are off somewhere to their right, in the dark behind the lights.

I didn't have a choice after the P.O.S.S.E. thing hit. I had to tell her about what happened to Akil—how it all went down, step by step. I told her how we're certain Leonard did wrong, we just can't prove it. She just listened and took it in. It was crazy.

I mean, I still can't quite believe she's here—or that she even set it up. See, Kurtis knew we couldn't do it at his place, or at the house of anyone he knew, so he asked if I might know someone, and I obviously don't, so I asked Aunt Blue and she called in a favor. Once she finally started talking after everything I told her, she hit me with a lot. She said she pre-ferred to be involved because *this whole endeavor needed some serious parental oversight.* Those are her words for it. She also let me know I'm a minor still (again), and I may be stupid, I may be getting myself into one great big awful mess, but I'm still family and I'm doing what I think is right. On that, she said, "I might not agree *with* you, but I believe *in* you, so I'll stand *by* you."

I don't think I've ever heard anything so good in all my life.

She said something else too, though. Something that threw me for the biggest loop ever. She said, *I'm your momma now.* The second she said it, I almost wanted to resist, like I was thinking I only ever had one, and if I had a new one that'd make my momma less important, but at the same time, I knew I wanted more than anything for it to be true. She lost a kid and I lost a mom. We're perfect for each other. We need each other the same amount. With all this running through my head again, I walk up to her by the workbench.

"You be sure to stand up for you, Grey Monroe," she says to me. "If you go down fighting for what you believe, and you're righteous, then it's no kind of loss. It's a seed you're planting, something that can grow into a victory."

I digest that before I say, "Kind of like the Freedom Riders?"

I've been thinking about the people who rode to desegregate the buses a lot lately. We're studying them in American history because we're doing our civil rights unit now.

"No, child, not like that at all. That's a different time, a heavier time. Do you even know that sit-ins started right up the road here? Morgan State students started that. There's proud history here in this city. Don't you even *think* of comparing yourself to those brave folks who fought racism so you can enjoy those hard-won freedoms today."

"I'm not comparing. I'm just saying. They were outlaws too, kind of."

"Outlaws because of unjust laws based on race, not because of *traffic* laws and driving too fast and out of control. Don't get it twisted now." She's got the tone in her voice that says, *you have a right to be wrong, but if you try arguing with me you'll be sorry.*

"Yes, ma'am" is all I say back.

"That's not to say this Leonard character didn't do wrong, or that it's easy being young, black, and male in this country, but I can't have you walking around thinking you're doing similar good against similar odds, because you're just not. Got it?"

"Yes, ma'am," I say again.

"That's better," she says. "How's your tummy doing anyway?"

"Good," I lie. It hurts like heck.

"Here, baby," she says, digging two chewable stomach pills out of a roll in her purse and handing them to me. "These should help."

This much I've learned since I moved here: Aunt Blue will give me a harder time than anybody on earth—*anybody*. But that's probably because she loves me more than anybody on earth too.

Somebody comes and gets me then, a skinny guy with glasses who needs me to sit down in the front of the camera so I can get dusted with makeup. Both Kurtis and I fought this at first, and I said we should just wear Akil masks, but Little Nate made the point that Cogland already put our faces out there, so why stop now? *Do you*, he said, *save the masks for the streets.* After that, he told us that with HD cameras it's important we don't look shiny and uneven, so we took his word for it, but we only did it after he'd done it first.

It's only me, Kurtis, and Little Nate doing this. All three of us are wearing our Akil T-shirts. Mike doesn't want to be on camera, Darryl neither, and Kurtis thinks that's a good idea, because we'll still need people with faces that aren't known.

I'm sitting on a stool to Kurtis's right when a girl tells me to close my eyes so she can swipe some dust over me.

"Close them tight," she says.

So I do. The brush glides over my forehead, cheeks, and nose, and then it's gone. "Okay," she says.

When I open my eyes, the interviewer is sitting there in front of us, her back to the big black camera. Actually, it's cameras.

It's two mounted together, one on top of the other. One is for close-ups and one for wide angle. That's what Little Nate said anyway. It's so they can shoot it in one go and edit it together later.

We get asked if we're ready and my stomach quivers like it's not, but that doesn't matter now.

After that, the red lights of the cameras come on, my stomach jolts, and I sit up as straight as I can.

42

THE INTERVIEW

The first question is about what Air Railroad actually is and what it means to us. Little Nate handles it even slicker than when he first told us. He's been thinking about it, honing it. He talks about Baltimore. The crime rate. Bad schools. Good people. But there's a serious lack of opportunity. No jobs. He calls it a city of survivors, hanging on.

But then he shifts gears, talking about how America is the land of the free and the home of the brave. How it always has been and always will be. But it's hard to be free from history and a legacy of slavery, racial fear, and the perceived inferiority of the entire black race. He goes on, saying that Air Railroad is a way of challenging preconceptions and stereotypes, breaking the invisible bonds that still exist in America by rising above them, and I find myself nodding along.

He says Air Railroad gives its members freedom to define themselves, rather than letting the world define them. He ends with, "I go to college. I'm making something of myself, and I can tell you true: We're not thugs; we're not drug dealers; we never have been; we think, we talk, we feel, we ride. We're *human*, and we just want to fly."

I'm still nodding at that when another question comes in. It's about Akil. Both Kurtis and Little Nate look to me.

I get choked up right then and they have to cut and go again. I tell them what happened that night, step-by-step. I tell them we were brothers because of what we'd been through. How Akil was the only one that understood where I was coming from. I mumble and stumble through it before I hit a point where I'm just angry—at myself, at the whole situation—and I let that hit my voice.

"Akil Williams," I say, "was the victim of policing overstepping its bounds. He wouldn't've been running if the police hadn't chased. He wouldn't've died if the police hadn't put him in that situation. They're the ones responsible for this. They're not on the right side of the law just because they wear badges."

Kurtis picks up on this and jumps right in, saying, "It's been open season on black men in America since before we were even a country. This isn't news to anybody. It's a *fact*. I'm not complaining about that. I'm just saying that's how it is, and though I accept it as true, it doesn't always have to be. Change has to come from somewhere and it starts with awareness. We're not here to fix anything because that's not up to us. We don't work in the government. We're just here to tell you how we see things, and that we got another stunt planned, one that just might kill us."

What comes right after that is an important moment. Kurtis told us about it before. He said how important resolve is right now. More important than anything in the whole interview. It's all for this moment when me, him, and Little Nate all look at the interviewer at the same time. We hold eye contact. We don't look away. We don't look scared. We look like we'll do anything.

"Trayvon Martin, Michael Brown, Akil Williams, and a thousand more you've never even heard of, much less cared about—black men die in America every day, every month, every year. We fly for them. The only thing that will be different here is that we're in control of our destiny. They had theirs taken away under tragic circumstances, but we get to choose when, where, and how we go. There's freedom in that, and if we die, we die with no regrets." Kurtis leans forward and for the briefest of moments, I think he's actually going to hit the interviewer. "*Believe* that."

He doesn't, of course, but she might think so too, because I see her shiver under her blue blazer.

That's how it starts.

That's when I know there's no going back. We have to push this as far as it will go.

43

STRUCK A CHORD

The interview didn't exactly go how we wanted when it aired. They cut stuff they shouldn't have. All the context Little Nate gave about how tough things are in Baltimore is gone, and they picked up from him saying, "Air Railroad is . . ." which is just stupid.

They also kept the bit in about me getting choked up and didn't even use the one where I said what I had to say! Instead, they switched to an interview with Akil's dad about what he thought about dirt bikers and of course he hates us. But after that you know they put Kurtis's promise about us maybe dying as the last bit. It was too raw to leave out, I guess.

All in all, I thought it was terrible, and Kurtis wasn't happy about it either. Little Nate said it wasn't a big deal, though, that it was just *marketing* and it didn't matter what they say, because we get to choose what our story is. Not them. Our channel on the MeTube is more important than what they say, and it'll always be that way.

Donations go crazy after the interview airs, though. Off-the-charts crazy.

It probably helped that Kurtis had Little Nate release the video of the jump off the Legg Mason building, all shot from Kurtis's perspective, as a sign of how serious we are about pushing limits. And people got it. Within twelve hours we're up over $500,000 before the stream starts to slow, and even then the number is chugging past $550,000 when it's time for breakfast. Kurtis and Little Nate slept over last night. Kurtis got the couch and Little Nate got the air mattress right next to him on the living room floor. Aunt Blue wouldn't have it any other way.

She's paranoid, thinking it's more likely people would rat out Kurtis and Little Nate since they've grown up here, but since I'm so new, it'd probably only be people at school who could, and even then, they don't know where I live. Besides, I think she wanted to get to know them better, partly out of curiosity, and partly out of seeing who I'm tying myself up with.

Nobody gets a chance to sleep in at Aunt Blue's house, not even guests. She's got us all rounded up by 5:30 a.m. because she's on a 7 a.m. shift but she wants us all to eat properly before she leaves. So she's scrambling up eggs in one pan and hash in another and I'm in charge of toast and juice, which I'm behind on because I can't stop yawning.

On the far side of the breakfast table, Little Nate and Kurtis lean against each other to stay propped up. Little Nate's more awake than Kurtis, though. He keeps hitting refresh on his phone.

The whole thing is surreal, a weird moment of calm in the middle of craziness, and that's when I think that maybe this is the eye of the storm—that, after this, we'll be whipped right back into the middle of it.

Aunt Blue says, "Don't be having that gadget out during breakfast, Nathan."

"Yes, ma'am," he says.

She turns. "What's it say now though?"

"Five hundred and fifty-five thousand, four hundred fourteen dollars and thirty-six cents," he says.

"Goodness, that sure is a lot of money. You've struck a chord with folks."

I have to admit I never thought Aunt Blue would get along with Kurtis and Little Nate, but it seems like all it took was some hospitality. She didn't do it just to be nice, though. Aunt Blue put herself in the conversation of what to do with the money, not because she wants it for herself, but because she doesn't trust us not to buy all kinds of bikes and cars and things. She wants us to give back to Baltimore. First and foremost. She wants to address the urban problems creating this bike culture in the first place.

"Also," she says, "you have to pay tax on this money. It isn't all yours. You need to give Uncle Sam his. We need to set that aside in a separate account, put it into some tax-free bonds so we can generate income on it to help us pay the bill when it comes in April next year. That's another reason why donations are such a good idea, not just because it's the right thing to do, to give back to your city and make it better, but because it lowers your tax burden. And have you looked into incorporating yet? Maybe even as a nonprofit?"

"Damn." Little Nate kicks my foot under the table. "Your aunt is *smart*."

"Don't you be using the *d* word in my house, Nathan."

"Sorry, ma'am," he says.

"And put that phone down now," she says as she maneuvers two hot pans onto their special trivets on the table.

He does. The hash keeps popping for a moment even after it's set down, just to let us know how hot and fresh it is. Aunt Blue hands one serving spoon to Little Nate and one to Kurtis.

"Don't let it get cold."

As they're digging in, my aunt says, "I just want to make it clear that I don't like what you all are up to. I don't like *any* of it. It's dangerous and it scares me to death that my Grey or either of you might end up like Akil. Now I know you had to say what you said about another crazy stunt for the TV, but I don't want any of that, and certainly no more talk of killing. Do I make myself clear?"

Everybody nods. Including me. But then I think about the plan, about flying, and I don't know how I'll tell her.

"But having said that," she says, "just because I don't like what you're doing doesn't mean I don't like you. Now let us pray."

She makes everybody grab hands and puts a good prayer out, but it's one with some guilt wrapped around it too. One about keeping us safe. One about guiding us to make the right choices, not just for us, but for everybody. After it's done, Little Nate's phone beeps and he looks at it.

"Nathan," Aunt Blue says.

"Sorry, Miss Blue," Little Nate says as he gets up from the table, "but I really have to check this."

He walks out into the hallway catching a look from Aunt Blue that I'm glad isn't aimed at me for once. I scoop two spoonfuls of hash onto my plate right next to a fluffy pile of yellow eggs, and then I mix them together. I'd prefer fried eggs and hash so I can mash the yolk and mix it with the meat and potatoes, but Aunt Blue cooks how Aunt Blue cooks and you either get used to it, or don't eat. Kurtis is right there with me, jamming his toast and looking as happy as I've ever seen him.

That doesn't last long, though, because Little Nate comes back in looking beat up. I'm the one that says "What's wrong?" first.

"Got a voice mail last night," he says. "Didn't get it till this morning. Stupid phone company. It's from Mike. He's in jail because P.O.S.S.E. came through his place last night and swooped him right up. Took his bikes, his laptop. They took everything. I was his one phone call from lockup."

Kurtis says, "That interview and video must've really got them hot. You better call Mon and tell her to get scarce, because her house is probably next—if it hasn't been hit already."

It's a small thing, but I think it's weird how I was thinking about it being Kurtis's house all along, when it was really Mon's. And I think how that makes sense, because I never heard about Kurtis having a job or anything.

"I'm on that, but there's something else you gotta see right now." Little Nate turns his phone around so Kurtis and I can read the screen.

It's an email submitted through the website. There's no name attached to it. Just an email address with a weird prefix. Letters and numbers only. No name there either.

I read it aloud. "I have proof of what pigs did to Akil. Do you want to see it?"

Even Aunt Blue's eyes get wide at that.

44

NO MORE BIKES

After breakfast and after Aunt Blue left for work, we wrote back to that email from the strange address, asking who the person is and what they got that proves Leonard did cause Akil's accident. We even signed it, "Kurtis, Air, & Little Nate." When we don't hear back for a couple hours we get to thinking we might never hear back from this guy. We start to worry if Cogland and P.O.S.S.E. maybe got him too.

Because it seems like just about everywhere in the city we even thought about going got hit last night.

Monika's house did get raided. Monika was there when it happened.

They scooped her up and held her till morning, but couldn't book her on anything, so she walked. When she got back, she found out the whole stash of Kurtis's bikes was gone. Two four-wheelers. An old-school Kawasaki Ninja. Three dirt bikes. All gone.

The entire garage got cleared out. On the concrete floor was a photocopy of a note stating that they had a witness statement that confirmed the vehicles were used in illegal activities, and if this was done in error, then all the owner had to do was show proof of ownership and could pick them up from city impound.

Little Nate says it's all a smart ploy. They're just trying to drag Kurtis out into the light to see if he's stupid enough to try to go down to impound to claim his property so they can arrest him for whatever else they have cooked up.

So the only thing we know now is that nobody can go back to their places.

Definitely not Kurtis. And probably not Little Nate. So everybody just gets cleaned up at Aunt Blue's. The smart thing is probably to stay indoors and not do anything.

But we can't help it.

I have preppy shirts and pants for me and Kurtis, but nothing to fit Little Nate.

There's only two options there: stay the same or do something drastic.

"Maybe we could go into Aunt Blue's closet," Kurtis says. "We could find you something there that would keep people from recognizing you."

"Man, *please*," Little Nate says. "I'm gonna wear what I wear. Wasn't my face on the news. Just on that interview."

He's right, but that doesn't mean it's the smartest. If the

knockos know us, they know him. It's that simple.

Kurtis says, "We're going downtown. There's a UFC fight on tonight. All kinds of people around. It's good cover for sure."

I know what he's saying. Pushing the plan up means doing reconnaissance and figuring out how we can safely pull off this stunt Kurtis promised everybody on television. Still, though, I need to know a little more than that, so I say, "How much we pushing this plan up anyway?"

Little Nate shrugs and says, "Soon as we can."

That's no kind of answer and he knows it. I say, "Which means what? I practice tomorrow? The day after?"

Kurtis laughs at that and he actually seems like himself again. I've been keeping an eye on him. Today he looks good, though. Eyes clear, not red. He's not looking sluggish. It's like he has his good days and his bad since I saw him throwing up. This is a good one, the best in a little while.

"This *afternoon*, man," he says to me.

I scoff because I think he's messing with me, but he's serious, I can see it. Little Nate is serious too.

I still don't get it. "How're we going to even find a place that will let me legally jump off a building?"

The room gets tight for a minute, everybody drawing in a breath and holding it before letting it go.

Little Nate busts up laughing first, and then Kurtis joins him. That's when I know I'm in trouble.

Little Nate almost has tears in his eyes when he says, "A building? Ain't no building, Air."

When I'm trying to figure out what he means by that, Kurtis says, "Don't worry. I know people."

It's a typical Kurtis answer, the kind that says not to ask anymore because you won't be getting a straight answer.

"Downtown first, though," he says. "*Then* we'll push you out of a plane."

45

DOWNTOWN

I'm twitching a little, thinking about skydiving, as we take the bus downtown and get off on South Howard, right by the Baltimore Arena. Even as we were getting close on the bus, we could all tell it was gonna be perfect cover. A couple hundred people are out walking the streets. Mostly younger people, or just a little older than us. It's exactly the right kind of camouflage. The cops that are out are only here to deal with traffic. They aren't scanning faces or anything.

I keep my eyes peeled, feeling like P.O.S.S.E. could be anywhere, even undercover.

The guys in the crowd all seem to be wearing black T-shirts with big white logos on them. We were worried they'd mostly be white people, but there's black folks too. There's couples. And even better, there's some sort of prefight gathering on

Hopkins Place, like a tailgate party or something. We cruise right past it and no one even gives us a second look. We've got about an hour before the undercard starts and the streets begin to clear and people go into the event. We need to use it right.

Hopkins Plaza is a good-sized bit of flat concrete right in front of the Federal Building, which is set about a football field away from West Baltimore Street. We walk right through. It's a little over a block from Hopkins Plaza to the Transamerica Tower.

"Jumping is not as different from riding as you might think," Kurtis says to me as we walk. "It's still about body control, about your mental focus and willingness to take it where no one else even thinks about going. It's just another challenge, Air. Something else to be beaten. It's what A.R. is all about. Only for those who live to be free."

"Only for those who live to be free," Little Nate says too. It sounds weird coming out of them like that. One after the other.

And it's hard not to think you can jump off a building when Kurtis tells you that you can. The fact is, though, I've never even skydived before. Forget BASE jumping. I only even know the term because Akil and I looked it up after saving Kurtis that one night. I know it means jumping off a fixed point (which I guess could be a building, or a mountain—anything that's not moving), and you do it with a parachute designed for quick openings. Other than that, I don't know anything about anything.

When we get to the Transamerica, we stop. Just being in its

shadow, it sure feels like the tallest building in the city. It hurts my neck looking up at it. It seems easier to make the leap from it, though. There's nothing much around it in terms of other tall buildings. There are multiple exit points from it, which is good. You could go southeast or southwest.

The only problem, everyone agrees, is the traffic lights on Pratt and Light, and on Pratt and Charles—and on that same side, slightly further down, a concrete bridge connecting the convention center to another building. All of those would need to be cleared by at least a few feet while coming down if you wanted to live.

"Well, let's walk the whole nine," Little Nate says. "Supposing we go off those opposite corners, that you both make it through your exits and come out clean. Where are you landing?"

All three of us turn 180 degrees and scan for landing spots.

"Near the harbor," Kurtis says, "near that old park. Nice and wide and flat."

"Straight down this street," I say, and look up to see the sign. "Straight down South Charles if we can avoid that pedestrian bridge."

Kurtis nods and tilts his head in one of his customary gestures that says it's doable, that it's just something to plan for.

On his phone, Little Nate types up this information in a little note file before copying and pasting it over into another file containing information on the tower. It's got forty floors. It's 529 feet high. After that, he plugs a little sensor into the end of his phone and takes a wind reading. Four miles per hour from the north/northeast.

I've never seen anything like it before. He's so organized, so prepared. And that's how I know they've been planning like crazy before even telling me. For what it's worth, it's good to see. It makes me relax a little and think maybe we can even do this.

Here's something most people don't understand about putting yourself out there: Doing stunts, it's actually not about adrenaline, not first and foremost. And it's not about risk either. If we wanted that, we'd stay on the streets and get mixed up in guns and drugs. There's far more risk waiting for us there than under any bike or jumping off any building.

With this stuff, the process is the thing. It's about looking at something impossible and finding a way to beat it, because breaking through barriers helps others see what can be done. If we shatter our limitations, maybe people will see they can shatter their own too.

I eye Little Nate's chart again as he's adjusting it and say, "How long you been thinking about doing this?"

"Planning for one person?" Little Nate eyes me. "About two months, way before you even. But with two people? Two different trajectories? Two different escape routes? Since right before we told you, pretty much."

Little Nate turns away from me and takes some quick video with his phone.

Sweeping a couple pans from the roof down South Charles

Street, and then we walk to Light and he does the same thing. That's all we really have time for. We have to go back to the bus stop as soon as he's done.

As the bus pulls in, Little Nate checks the Air Railroad email on his phone. "Still no reply on that email," he says. "Maybe they really did get him." Kurtis shrugs and we get back on the bus for home.

"Or it's something else," Kurtis says when we're settling in. "It could be the knockos trying to fish for us. Setting up a meet might actually mean walking right into an ambush."

We all sit quiet after that.

It didn't really seem a possibility until now, but when you've got public contact information on a website that anybody can see—including the people that most want to catch you and arrest you—then anything can happen.

Anything at all.

46

LEARNING TO FALL

That afternoon, we're in Churchville, Maryland—11,000 feet above the ground. I can only barely see it below me, between clouds. I know it's green, though. The greenest place I've ever seen. And it's quilted out into patches that aren't exactly squares or rectangles but are like every other kind of shape there is. Puzzle-piece shapes with legs and cutouts that look like cartoon mouths. Amoeba shapes tangling themselves up with clumps of trees that must go on for miles.

It's funny how it's impossible to see these kind of land patterns from the earth, the borders and the way the shapes fit together, sometimes mashed up against each other—well, not funny like a joke, but more like true. Perspective needs distance.

I've never been up in a plane like this before, not one I was right about to jump out of, and my heart won't stop trying to pound out of my chest. It feels the fear and it's just reacting. But if losing my momma taught me anything, it's that fear is better than nothing. The same goes double for Akil. I'd rather be afraid than numb. Every time.

And I'd rather jump than sit around and wait to be arrested.

Things have been moving so fast since the interview. I *haven't* had time to think about anything, but maybe that's for the best. Act. Don't think. Keep moving.

I feel the strap beneath my arm tighten up real quick, like a blood pressure cuff.

The rhythm of the engine propeller thumps through me as the skydiving instructor checks the tightness of my harness and yells into my ear.

He says, "Tight enough for you?"

I nod, but not at him since he's behind me. I'm not sure if he got that, so I put my thumb up to let him know.

"Good, man," he says. "Good!"

His name's Chad. He gave me his life story within two minutes of meeting him.

He's from California but has been living in Maryland for a few years because his girlfriend got a job out here. He's an only child, grew up in San Clemente, and he's in his mid-thirties with a chin beard going. He is exactly the kind of white guy that never thinks about what it means to be a white guy ever. To him, it's just how it is, not something other people try to decide for you. The way he talks to people and calls them *bro*, he's the type of person I avoid. At school. Anywhere. But the coolest thing about the Internet is that it connects you to people you'd never be connected to otherwise. Chad is one of those. The best kind. Because he hooks you up with stuff.

He idolizes Kurtis. He'd seen what Kurtis could do on the MeTube and reached out through Little Nate to invite him up to skydive months ago. He taught him to jump and chute (that's what Chad calls it) about the time I first moved here. In fact, as we were putting our suits on in the locker room, Little Nate showed Chad the video of Kurtis landing his jump off the Legg Mason.

Chad looked impressed, but made sure to get his dig in. "Need to work on that landing, bro."

"Work?" Kurtis put on a face like he was confused. "That was textbook. Just like you taught me."

"I taught you to fall better than that."

I'm thinking about those words as they get ready to open the door to my right.

And I guess that's what this is for me, learning to fall.

When the side door gets opened on the plane, Kurtis is first to it. He's got experience, and he gets to go solo. I've never done this before and yet, I have to go solo too, because otherwise there's no way I can do it myself when it really matters.

Better this than sitting in a jail cell.

Kurtis lines up and faces me before going out backward. *Whoosh*. Just like that.

He's gone. I see his body drop away and my stomach spins inside me.

After that, Chad nudges me forward. He holds his hand up and I grab it.

That's the plan. We jump together from 2,500 feet. He'll let go when he sees I'm okay, and I have to watch him for when to pull my chute. I got a quick course on the ground in how to pull and steer but this is stupid crazy and probably illegal and Chad could lose his license if anyone found out I've never jumped before—

Right then is when the calm hits me. I feel it like a hand on my shoulder.

I imagine it's Akil's. I imagine it's there to remind me that this isn't the craziest thing I've ever done. Riding blind was that, and always will be. And this? At least I'm not racing into a void.

At least I can see the ground coming.

Chad shouts in my ear through the wind rushing past, "You ready for some real air, Air?"

He barks a laugh after that, like it's easy being him and living his life because he's a really fun, easygoing guy that always cracks himself up.

He doesn't give me time to think.

He says, "One, two, three."

And on *three*, he jumps and I go with him, out into the wind.

47

BEAT THE WORLD

Chad throws his trailer chute almost right away, so I do the same. I don't know what I thought falling from this high up would feel like, but it feels like being weightless. My arms spread-eagle out to my sides like it's the most natural position and then the wind just holds me up.

Or it feels like it anyway.

I know I'm falling. I feel the pressure of it, but it's like my brain doesn't know. My face does, though. My cheeks try to peel all the way back to my ears.

Free fall is supposed to be less than a minute. But I lose track of time.

I just know I'm supposed to hold my arm tight and steady as Chad flexes his whole body, lets go of my hand, and pushes off from me—getting far enough away for us both to pull our chutes without getting tangled.

I hope anyway.

Thoughts race each other in my head—good ones like *if I can blind-ride I can do this* and *nothing more natural than falling* compete with bad ones like *maybe my chute won't open* and *I'm going to die by going* smack *in a field* and *will I black out before I get there?*—but when Chad pulls his chute, I pull mine.

Gravity jumps up and meets me right where I am as I get shot up into the sky.

It feels like I got popped out of a cannon. It's so violent and fast that I'm sure I left all my thoughts back where I used to be, because right then, the only thing that matters is what's above me.

I look up as the parachute flaps open in slow motion, like the wind's unfolding it. That's when I feel scared again.

I hear brackets and buckles and ropes and straps straining.

It snaps me back into reality. And into danger. Because now I have to land.

Something could happen between now and the ground if we didn't fit my harness right. I go through the beginner's landing instructions in my head again: Ride the wind but stay stable and balanced. Keep my core tight. Keep my legs roughly the same length and same width apart. Hold my steering handles the same length and width away from my body. Don't try to turn at all. Just stay stable and ride the line down.

So I do.

And I'm good until I get close, until I see the ground looking inevitable. Fifty feet. Twenty. Ten. The earth comes at me fast, like it's sprinting at me, streaking to a blur, and I'm standing still. I hold my breath then, and reach out to touch down with both feet at the same time just like I was told, and when that works, I try to run, but I'm going too fast and I tumble a few times and land flat on my back, knocking my wind out, as my chute deflates around me.

It takes me a moment to gather my breath back, but my legs work. My arms work. When I get up with some grass in my mouth, I have a whole new appreciation for Kurtis landing on an asphalt road.

The first thing I do after that is look up at the airplane, at how it's a speck above me, and I can't believe I did it. The adrenaline's so big in me, I scream. Just one long *fuck you* to the sky and the land and the trees. To everything that could have killed me but didn't. I feel every blood vessel in my head. And when I breathe, I feel every single centimeter of my lungs inside me.

I feel like I just beat the world.

That feeling gets bigger when Kurtis and Chad come running over whooping and yelling how they couldn't believe it and how good I was.

We do three more jumps, one right after the other. On the last one, I work the parachute a little and try some very shallow turns, pulling them off without managing to wreck myself.

"You're a natural," Chad says when we're back on the ground.

After that, we go into the locker room where I get a surprise: the BASE parachute I've been jumping with is mine now. It's a gift from Chad. After I get told that, I have to drill to make sure I can do all that needs to be done on my own. I go through the protocol of setup and teardown, from straps to pop, packing it back up, and starting all over again. I end up putting it on and taking it off five times. By the third time, I've got it cold, but I still get told to do it again at home when I get there and Kurtis has to watch to make sure I do it right. Chad says good-bye then, but not before I thank him.

"No problem, bro," he says.

In the parking lot, Little Nate's pacing by the van when we get there and load up.

He looks about as happy as a wet cat.

"We got a meeting with the mystery man," he says.

Kurtis says, "Where?"

"Faidley's, in Lex Market. A couple hours."

Kurtis makes a face. "He picked that?"

"Nah," Little Nate says, "I did. Feels to me like a special-occasion place like that would be exactly where they wouldn't expect us to go."

"In public is good," Kurtis says, and shrugs his bag up further onto his shoulder.

"I'm second-guessing it, though," Little Nate says. "I mean, that's downtown, awfully close to police."

"Don't," Kurtis says, like once he tells you not to do something it's the easiest thing in the world not to.

That's when I jump in. "What's Faidley's?"

Kurtis and Little Nate turn to give me the exact same look at the exact same time: *How could you be so unbelievably stupid?*

48

A TRADE

It's only a half hour back to Baltimore from Churchville, so we get to Lexington Market early and post up. Even before we get there, I get told that Lex Market is an enclosed public market that takes up a whole city block between Eutaw and Green. (When I heard Kurtis say it, I thought it was like *Utah*, but then when I saw it spelled *Eutaw*, I thought it was about perfect for how Baltimore folks talk, dragging their *u*'s out.)

Part corner, part cracked-out market is what Little Nate calls the Lex. It's been at its location forever. Eighteenth century apparently. I see the corner aspect that Little Nate mentioned as soon as we walk inside. There's kind of a public square in the middle, with knots of black people around it and inside it, carrying on conversations next to a book fair that nobody seems to be buying from.

"Keep your wallet close," Kurtis says to me as we move through. "I'm not saying it's about to be taken, but I'm not saying it's not either."

Faidley's Seafood feels like a little ship floating inside Lex Market. The wall says it was founded in 1886. Its blue metal ceiling is all beams and rivets. On my right as we walk in from the market, freezers sit side-by-side along a whole wall like a row of giant silver teeth. The whole thing is on a slant too, with doors to the outside a good few feet higher than the market entrance. In the middle of it all is a raw bar that serves oysters. Crowding up on it are old-timers with their hats the right way around. There's pretty much a divide between them. If they're white, they're talking Orioles' baseball. If they're black, it's Ravens' football. Here and there beside them, leaning on the bar or on the nearby tall tables, are girls in skinny jeans hovering over oysters.

Kurtis takes up a table past the raw bar, about twenty feet away, so we're not all together. So we're not one big target. We figure if somebody's approaching, they'll approach him since he's the most recognizable of any of us. Even with a hat down low.

I get told to stand in the corner and be on the lookout for people coming in and out. The first order of business is to see if anybody looks like cops, but the only white people in here are old or tourists with mustaches and hats with feathers in them. I scan the specials board. Smelt is on there, fresh and frozen. Cutlass fish. Apparently raccoon is in season too. Muskrat goes in-season on the first of June. Most people here aren't ordering anything to take away, though. They're eating.

There's all kinds of people here. Asian. White. Black. It's a good feeling seeing that. I don't feel as awkward, or like I stand out at all. And the funny thing is, it's not something I even notice until it's right in front of me. It lasts for a good minute until Little Nate walks up and slides two plates onto the table, one in front of me.

"Can't come all the way here and not get some jumbo lump," he says.

There's a crab cake on my white throwaway plate. It's light brown, the size of a fist, and sitting on top of a bed of lettuce and tomatoes. Next to it is a packet of saltine crackers. It doesn't look like any crab cake I've ever seen because it's mounded, not flat like a patty.

Little Nate elbows me. "You gonna eye it or eat it?"

I fork some up and give it a taste—damn, it's fluffy like a warm, crab-tasting cloud with just the right amount of fry and a hint of mayo. As I'm forking another bite in, a big guy approaches Kurtis from the side. He's wearing a denim jacket, and it isn't until he turns that I see it's Darryl.

Darryl says but six words to Kurtis, puts a slip of paper on the table, and leaves. I'm wondering what he wrote when a little boy in a black baseball cap comes up to me and says, "I got something in my hand you probably want."

When I hear the voice, though, it hits me and I feel a little sick. That same voice screamed at Leonard when we were in the street, standing over Akil. It'll be with me for the rest of my life. But when I look at his eyes, I know immediately that it's not a boy at all. It's a *girl*.

She's probably not much older than me. I can't tell how old from a glance though. Maybe Akil's age, seventeen or eighteen. I wince. The age Akil *used to* be.

Her skin's black like hot chocolate with no milk. Brown black. To show me she is who she's supposed to be, though, she flashes what looks like a silver USB drive in her hand. The kind of device a video could be on. Or photos.

Little Nate talks to her but doesn't turn to face her, like he learned it from somebody trying to be slick on TV. "What you got there?"

"Nobody asked you nothing, fat boy. Keep your mouth shut or I walk. I'm talking at Air."

Little Nate sniffs and nods for me to go on.

My mouth goes dry as I say, "What do you want for it?"

I'm trying to catch Kurtis's eyes but he's just standing where he is, looking down.

My heart's really going now. Smacking on my ribs. I can't lose this and have it be on me. I can't be this close to proof and have it slip. Especially not if it shows Leonard's guilty. I'll agree to anything right then. Anything.

"A trade," she says.

"What for what?"

"I give this to you," she says, "I'm Air Railroad for life."

Little Nate keeps his stare on the raw bar but he crosses

his arms. I feel him do it beside me, and it's like I know his answer.

"That's not my call to make," I say. "We've all got to decide."

It isn't exactly true, but I don't know what else to say. I'm just buying time for Kurtis to turn, to notice us.

"It'll have to be," she says, "because I walk in thirty seconds."

I smile at that, but I'm wincing inside.

"I could lie to you," I say. "What's to stop me?"

"Nothing," she says, "but you won't."

"Then just tell me why you want in. I at least need to hear that."

"Only for those who live to be free, right?" She wrinkles her brow up and when she does that, I see she's got big brown eyes and a scar down her cheek that looks like a little hook. "Well, that's me. I don't know no other way to live. You'll just have to take my word on that."

"All I have to do is say you're in?"

"All you have to do is say I'm in," she says. "You only got ten seconds."

Little Nate's trying to elbow me but I ignore it.

"Nine," she says, looking to the specials boards. "Eight."

"You're in," I say.

She grabs my hand, opens it, and pushes the USB into my palm. It's a little sweaty, which is weird because I didn't figure she was nervous until just then.

"Hey," I say as she's turning, "what should I say your name is when Kurtis asks?"

"Ellah," she says, "like the singer, but with an *h* on the end of it."

I can't help being curious. "That got a meaning to it?"

"Everything's got a meaning to it," she says.

And then she smiles at me, a smile that reaches up to her eyes and sparks them like sun glinting off a windshield, before she turns away for real this time, and weaves herself through a tour group and out the door.

49

FAR AWAY BUT COMING CLOSER

We're in the van, in a parking garage across the street from Lex Market, when we all decide we can't drive back to Aunt Blue's, we have to see what's on Ellah's USB first. No choice, really. I can't get her smile out of my head. It's not that it was pretty, it was just so confident. Like, she thought I was going to appreciate whatever I found on the drive, that it would be worth it. There was something else, though, too. Relief. Joy. I recognized it as soon as I saw it because it's how I felt about meeting Kurtis for the first time too, and even more so when me and Akil became a part of what he was doing.

Kurtis was angry she didn't come to him, and he wondered why she came at me instead, but I think he was mostly angry that he didn't notice until we told him how it went down—and the deal I had to make—before putting the USB in his hand.

"I guess we'll have to see if this's worth having some no-account hood rat hanging around then, huh?"

That's what he had to say about that, and it bothered me a little.

Little Nate pretty much said what I was thinking, though. "If she's 'no-account,' then what are you? She sure got the drop on us. You think we couldn't use somebody like that? And hasn't Mon been saying we need more girls? Looks like win-win to me. Who cares if she can ride? She can learn."

"She called you a fat ass, though," I said.

"So? That wasn't throwing shade. She was talking facts. My ass *is* fat." He laughed and slapped at it just so we could hear the *thump* of it. "Solid too."

I couldn't help laughing at that. Little Nate is a funny dude when he wants to be.

Kurtis was still a little mad, though, and he stayed mad all the way to the van.

The day might just be turning bad for Kurtis. He looks fragile around the eyes and he's squinting more, like he's got a headache.

But how he's acting right now, it's like he thinks he didn't get his proper respect and he's jealous. Maybe Ellah just didn't see Kurtis when she walked in? I can't help myself wondering if it's something more, though. If Kurtis is worried I'm getting just as big as him even though he set me up to be that way from the start, starring in stunts and all that, but maybe it backfired because there was no Air Railroad until Air came along.

I wonder if he regrets naming me a little. Like with how my name is in the group name now, people might think it's mine. I haven't wondered much until now why he decided to make this more than just the Kurtis show. That trips me out for a bit.

It's still messing with me when we get to the van and settle ourselves in the back where the bikes used to be. Little Nate busts out his laptop and after the screen warms up, he plugs the USB in the side. A square icon appears on his desktop and he double-clicks it.

There's only one file on the drive and it gets clicked. The video player jumps up on the screen and Little Nate makes sure it takes over everything when it starts playing automatically. It's a straight up-and-down cell phone camera video.

A cat pops up on the screen. A white cat under a streetlamp at night. The picture is grainy and fuzzy.

Little Nate says, "What?"

Kurtis is on it too. "I think we just got *got*."

That cat licks its paw as the camera pans out a little.

I say, "Does it have sound?"

We all lean in.

"Yeah," Little Nate says.

Kurtis sniffs, like *whatever*. "Turn it up then."

Little Nate does. He gives it three taps.

And when he does, I can hear a bike engine. Far away but coming closer. The camera zooms all the way out when that happens, leaving the cat under the streetlamp, looking tiny. The camera swings around, probably looking for the source of the sound, but there's nothing. It goes up and down the street.

That's when I see the truck. Double-parked.

"Oh shit," I say. I can't help myself. "That's the street."

Kurtis rubs his eyes and squints at the screen. He leans forward and he breathes in but doesn't let it out. The engines get louder. That familiar whine comes closer.

And the person aiming the camera knows where it's coming from now because it goes to the right and points at the corner. Even better, it goes to landscape mode because whoever is taking it must turn the phone to widescreen in their hands.

And when that happens, you can see a chunk of the next street and one headlight coming fast and taking the corner.

It's Akil.

Right behind him. Right on top of him. Is the cop car.

50

RODNEY-KING IT

As the cop car and Akil both go around the corner, we hear the patrol car's engine rev up when it's taking the turn tight—almost like it's aiming at the back tire of Akil's bike—and in that moment, I realize it is. It *is* aiming. And when he hits Akil's tire, the cop car speeds up, driving Akil into the back gate of the truck, sending him airborne.

In the van, all three of us jump as Ellah's voice hisses, "Lord Jesus!" Akil's body goes so far he doesn't even land on screen.

"Oh my god," I say. I don't even mean to. It just comes out. And once it does, it keeps going. I'm repeating it.

Over and over.

Because if I don't, I'm going to be sick.

Kurtis puts a hand on my shoulder and squeezes. That's the only thing that stops me, because I'd keep going if he didn't.

Tires screech after that. The cop car brakes in the middle of the street. Its siren stops. But there's another whine coming.

And it's got to be my bike.

It's got to be me.

But we don't see my headlight coming, because whoever's got the camera is running downstairs. It's one of those jumpy runs you can't even look at when you're watching because it's moving too much, but then a door is open and the camera goes outside and its flash pops on, throwing a white halo of light onto the street where Akil is down and Leonard is standing there and in front of him is me.

I'm watching me on the screen, me staring down Leonard like I mean to kill him. The camera gets closer.

Little Nate turns the audio all the way up.

Leonard's apologizing to me.

And then he looks around, straight at the camera.

That's when Ellah yells, and it's so loud over the speakers, "I saw what you did! I saw you speed up and hit him!"

And in the second Leonard steps back, I'm saying, "You're gonna regret this shit. You just birthed another level."

I'm about to hit STOP then, but the screen cuts to black. That's all there is.

We need a moment after that. Some long, not-saying-anything moments. We know what we just watched. We know how it happened now.

Not only did Leonard chase, but he aimed to smash Akil's back wheel right into that truck. I'm no lawyer, but bumping somebody into a truck that kills them has to be about as illegal as it gets.

Little Nate agrees. We all do. People need to *see* this.

He has to download the video from the stick drive to his desktop in order to take the USB out and then put in his wireless stick in the same slot so he can upload it to YouTube under our account.

It makes sense. It's the widest possible audience we can reach. So we're going to Rodney-King it.

And let people see how evil Leonard is for themselves.

Little Nate gets to the standard YouTube upload page and taps the title out on the keys. *Breaking News*, he writes. *Evidence of P.O.S.S.E. killing Akil.*

Kurtis turns the keyboard toward himself. He deletes the last bit and writes Proof Baltimore Police Killed Akil Williams before pushing it away from him.

Toward me.

Little Nate nods at that, so I get working on the description. I'm a six-finger typer (just my first two fingers and thumbs), but I'm mad, so it comes out in one fast spill.

On April 2, 2014, Akil Williams got chased by BPD and was hit at high speed by a car driven by Patrolman Leonard. This is the video of what actually happened that night. It's the video no dirty Baltimore cop wants you to see. Which is exactly why you should. Spread the word. Tell everybody. Show everybody.

When I'm done, I let out a long breath, sag my shoulders, and say, "Is that okay?" They've both got wide eyes in response.

For how long, I don't know.

"I mean," Kurtis says, "I'd've been way more nasty. Nobody on the Internet writes that good. I'd've been like *shit*-this and *motherfucker*-that. And lots of exclamation points. I'd put a mess of them in."

Maybe it's not the time to make a joke, but maybe it is. I laugh at that, and then I feel guilty about it.

"Yeah," Little Nate says, "needs way more curses. But it's good, though. Like, informative. People might even take it serious. And that's good. Because it's as serious as it gets."

Kurtis nods and moves the mouse over to the SUBMIT button. He looks at us real seriously then and says, "Post?"

His skin looks almost grey in the blue light of the computer screen. Little Nate's does too. I'm nodding. We all know this is a moment you don't turn back from, and we're glad, because we don't want to turn back from it.

We run toward it. We *take* it.

That's how it feels when Kurtis pushes the button.

51

WHERE YOU NEED TO END UP

Tomorrow is the day. It has to be. There's no more time to waste. We all decided in the van. For Akil. I'm feeling the weight of it—still up in my room, still awake, even though Kurtis and Little Nate are asleep downstairs—when Aunt Blue knocks on the door and asks to come in. I say she can. The door opens and she spots *The Freedom Box* straightaway. The book is next to me on the bed since I just finished reading it. And maybe she has other things on her mind, but she wants to know what I think of it first.

She says, "Not half bad, is it?"

"It's better than that," I say, and I kind of hold there.

So of course she calls me out on it.

"But?" She cranes her neck. "There's something you don't like about it?"

"It's a good book. Better than good," I say. "The pictures are really great."

"There you go again," Aunt Blue says. "But?"

"Because it's a book for kids, it's only the skeleton of the story. I wanted to go deeper. I wanted to know how it felt to Henry when he stretched for the first time after getting out of that box, what it felt like to him to be in freedom for the first time."

She tilts her head. "That's fair. But did it make you think about what I said, though? Do you know where you need to end up? You've got to know how you're setting yourself up and what's next. You've got to plan beyond just the next stunt. You've got to plan for *years*."

"But you can't plan everything," I say.

"Of course you can."

"But then what if it doesn't happen?"

"Make a new plan. Adjust."

"And what if I'm already adjusting in the moment? When I ride, I'm figuring out as I go. I'm flowing. Is that so bad?"

"Young man, if that's not the logic for anybody whoever ended up in a ditch, than I don't know what is."

You can't beat Aunt Blue at word games. She'll chew you right up. I've been finding that out every day for months. Now I just know that I have to be true to what I think and feel. That's all I can do.

"I belong to something, Aunt Blue. Something real."

"Oh, I can see that. It's *too* real for my liking." She snorts.

"Personally, I'd have preferred the chess club."

I make a face.

"But that's not you, is it?" She smiles sadly as she picks up the Valkyrie key chain on my dresser and turns it over in her palm. "It wasn't your momma either. You're more her than any of them. Not Jamar. Not the twins. You're her reflection."

That hits me. My voice goes quiet when I say, "I've never heard you say that before."

She sets the key chain back down, gently, exactly where she found it. "Well, it's true. I've never had cause to say it until now, and never have I felt it so strongly since you came to stay here. It's like seeing her all over again, how you crinkle your nose up, how you won't eat mushrooms."

I never thought how much of my momma comes out in me on a daily basis.

Knowing I got her mannerisms and gestures makes me happy. Makes me feel like she's not totally gone.

"Good has to come from this, Grey," Aunt Blue says. "It *has* to. That money you got coming in can change peoples' lives. It can meet an awful lot of ends. But none of that is worth it if . . ." She falters there as she's talking. Her voice goes out from underneath her. My strong aunt, the toughest person I've ever met, is having trouble finishing what she's saying.

I take her hand and hold it. She turns her head halfway away from me, like she doesn't need me doing that, but she appreciates it.

"None of it is worth it," she says again, "if it costs me you.

That's why I can't give any kind of blessing on this stunt of yours, or any stunt. I'd forbid it too, if it'd stop you. But you are your momma's boy, and you'd be gone the second I turned my back."

"I don't need you to say yes," I say. "I just need you to not say no."

Aunt Blue gets to rubbing her temples. "Do you even know what you're asking?"

"I think I do," I say. "I'm asking for trust."

"Have you earned it though? Sneaking out? Coming home late? Riding fast and dangerous and putting not just yourself at risk, but other people too?"

"No." I feel small just saying it.

"You've seen the price of it already, Akil laying up dead in the funeral parlor, and *still* you want to do it. You aiming to put me through another of those too, but this time with you in the casket?"

I stare at the book beside me. The little boy on the cover is staring at the ceiling. "I'm *responsible* for you," she says. "Do you get that?"

Sure, I get it. And in order to get away from her talking about me being a minor again, I say, "Aren't we both responsible for me?"

She sighs at that, and for me it's an opportunity to tell her one last time where I'm coming from.

"I need to do it for me," I say, "and for people like me, people that don't even know they can have a purpose till it finds them.

I'm doing it for Akil. Doing it for people that got done like he did." I stop there because the last one, the one I have on my heart, is tricky. But I know I just have to say it anyway. "And I'm doing it for Momma too. She never had the—"

Aunt Blue jumps all over that one. She's got tears in her voice, but they haven't reached her eyes yet. "Don't you say that. Don't you dare. It's not fair. This is *not* for your momma. This is for you. And if you stopped being selfish for one minute, you'd see that."

"But if I do it and I use the money to help Baltimore folks, is it still for me?"

"It is if something happens to you," she says.

I don't know what to say to that, so I don't say anything. The last thing I want is Aunt Blue sitting at my funeral, but everything we built up after Akil went away will be gone if we don't go forward with this. It's no kind of choice. We said we'd do something on national TV, so we have to do it. We have to come through and be true to our words, show we aren't scared, show we don't need permission. When you're visible, that's just how it is. If we don't have integrity now, nobody will believe in us again.

Momma would've understood that. Aunt Blue does too, even if she'd never say so.

"My answer is still no," Aunt Blue says, and it's the last word too, because she goes right after it's out of her mouth, closing the door real hard behind her too, like an exclamation point on the end of the sentence.

52

MOMENTUM

Come morning, the house has a hush to it. Kurtis and Little
Nate are downstairs but I can't hear them. They've been good
houseguests and I know because Aunt Blue hasn't complained
even once. That's mainly because they clean up after themselves in the morning, deflating the air mattress and putting
the couch back the way it was.

Aunt Blue's out at the market getting groceries for the week.
She doesn't have work today. I feel bad she doesn't even know
today's Jump Day, but she couldn't or it'd never go right.

I'm extra aware of everything right now. How the sheets
feel on me when I get out from under them. How the com-
forter feels on my fingertips as I make the bed. The heat of the
shower. The cool of the tub on the bottom of my feet before it
warms up.

Steam opening up my sinuses. I don't know if this is normal, but maybe this is how it goes on a day when it could be your last on earth.

That's how it is for me anyway.

Outside my window, clouds stretch across the whole sky and I have to sit there for a minute and just look at them. It looks like an upside-down blanket. Like the sky got tucked in last night and hasn't woken up yet. The whole time I'm looking the clouds don't hardly move. Which is more than likely good because the less wind there is, the better. It's one of the few things we're not in charge of. That one's on God.

Everything else, though? I've done my best to lock it down. We've been talking back and forth about it, but the plan is pretty much locked down now.

1. Get the parachutes. That got checked off in Churchville, and they're already in the van in some sealed delivery boxes, which brings me to the next one.

2. Get delivery driver uniforms. We had to get these from a supply store that had blanks in stock. Ours are light blue. It's what I get dressed in. The button-up shirt matches the pants, and we even got hats too, which is a nice touch. That was all Little Nate. That dude is good with detail and design. Real good. He even got us patches with the fake logo of our fake company on it. It's a royal blue and white logo and the words *Air Express* on a van with little

wings on it and lines behind the back wheels so it looks like it's hauling.

I leave my wallet on the dresser, but I grab my momma's key chain on the way downstairs and I button it into the shirt pocket that's over my heart. It's heavy there, but a good kind of heavy. It's how I'll keep her with me today, no matter what happens.

When I walk into the kitchen, Kurtis has already showered and he's wearing his Air Express uniform too. We can't help smiling at each other. And Little Nate makes us put the final touch on, white gloves, before taking a picture of us together like it's Halloween or something.

Before the shutter clicks, Kurtis says to me, "You almost look grown up."

"You too," I say.

I don't eat much for breakfast. I'm too nervous. All I can get down is half a bowl of dry cereal. No milk.

Little Nate hears me crunching and says, "How can you even eat it like that?"

"It's like chips," I say. "Almost."

Little Nate shrugs, which is fine, because I'm not really in the mood for conversation and neither is he. We're in our own heads now. Going through mental checklists. For me, it's the rest of the plan.

3. Access Transamerica Tower with our parachutes packed in delivery boxes. Kurtis says he has an inside man for this, and that I have to trust him.

4. Once we're in, we go straight to the roof in the elevator. We have to walk the last floor and change in the stairwell.

5. Jump from the roof, with Kurtis going one direction and me going another.

6. Survive it. This is the one that's no kind of guarantee, especially for me.

7. Get picked up. Two teams. All hands on deck. Mon and Mike have been released. Kurtis says BPD doesn't have the budget to track them, but it's not worth it taking that chance. We got some new-old people in for Kurtis's team, basically the guys with Mike and Darryl that night of the Legg Mason jump, and some new people in for my team. Somebody Kurtis doesn't want to trust just yet, but I do. Ellah.

I write a note for Aunt Blue before we're out the door and leave it on the kitchen table. It's not much, just has a hotel address on it. It's the place I'll be if everything goes right tonight. I figure she'll be there or she won't.

It's the calmest things will be all day.

Because the second we walk out the door, it's nothing but spy-style. Little Nate gets in through the back double doors of the van and shuts them. Kurtis drives. I'm shotgun.

On our way to the tower I say, "We know how the Leonard video's doing yet?"

"There was an article in the *Sun* about it," Little Nate says from the back. "Page two, but still."

That's just crazy. I say, "Overnight? Really?"

"Yup," he says. "It's getting shared like wild. ACLU of Maryland tweeted about it this morning too, and now their national is gonna push for an investigation into Leonard, but we'll see."

I think about that for a second. It's ridiculous how fast it's all happened. But then something else occurs to me. "Since when do you read the newspaper anyway?"

Little Nate looks at me like I'm slow. "I get alerts sent to my email, man. Certain things get mentioned online, search engines find it and let me know about it. That article was the best, though. It quoted the district attorney saying he wanted to look into the Leonard thing, and you *know* that's good. I'm not going to get my hopes up that Leonard will actually get punished, but momentum is building."

53

EVERYBODY WILL KNOW IT WAS US

By the time we get to the Transamerica, nobody's talking. I'm still watching the sky. It hasn't changed. Still grey. My kind of day. No rain either. And that's even better. I'm real curious about wind speed now, but there's nothing I can do about that.

I go through the plan in my head. Over and over.

It's funny how Aunt Blue basically taught me how to do that and I had to act like I never think about what I'm doing when we talked last night, that I just do something, and she thinks that's perfect logic for ending up dead in a ditch. She's not wrong. Still, it wouldn't have made her feel any better if I told her this had been planned since before the interview.

The part of the plan that's sticking to me now is how I have to jump toward South Charles and manage to miss that pedestrian bridge. It's the safest jump, though. Not into traffic. Not really. Kurtis got that one. I trip on that for a while and we're on West Baltimore Street before I know it.

Kurtis says to me, "You ready?" I can only nod.

On our last scout through, we noticed delivery vans pulling up on the South Charles side and putting their blinkers on, so that's what we do. Kurtis and I get out at the same time, shut our doors, and roll to the back where Little Nate pops out and hands us our packages complete with packing slips we created from a template we found on the Internet, then we step up onto the curb, looking dead ahead.

Business people in their suits and ties pass us but they don't spare a second look. We're invisible now. In the best way. Because we need to be. Uniforms can be useful. Nobody suspects a jump right off the tallest building in Maryland during daytime so everybody can see it, so everybody will know it was us.

The lobby is smaller than the rectangular building. It's a little glassed-in square underneath the four concrete pillars on the corners. You don't have to get buzzed in or anything. You can walk right up to it and go in through spinning doors. I let Kurtis go first, and then I wait for the next space to come up and push in. By the time I get through, Kurtis is already heading straight to the security desk where a guard I recognize is waiting for us.

54

UP

It's Darryl in a big navy blazer and a red tie. He looks glad to see us too. He breaks out in a smile before composing himself and pushing a clipboard our way.

"Right on time," he says. "We're right in his window."

I don't ask whose window. I just study the clipboard. It has a standard sign-in form on it, I guess. Name. Company. Date. Time in. Time out. At the end of it is a little initial box for the guard to show he witnessed it.

Kurtis grabs the pen at the top of the board and writes his name in the log as *Leonard*, the company as *Air Railroad*. He puts the date as today's, the time in as now, and the time out as ten minutes from now.

He hands me the pen and I do the same thing, but I sign my name as *Cogland*.

It's amazing how much you can learn about buildings at the library: Who the tenants are and where they are. How much they pay per square foot. But more importantly, how the building works. Blueprints. Roof access points. Security layouts.

By now, Little Nate will have sent out a blast to every single organization that asked to interview us. The TV companies. The newspapers. The high-powered Internet blogs with a bunch of readers.

The email will have a street address in it.

This address: 100 Light Street, Baltimore, Maryland 21202.

It says something will happen here in fifteen minutes. It doesn't say what. It just suggests being in the courtyard on the Pratt Street side.

Fifteen minutes isn't a lot of time for anyone to get anywhere with a camera, even if you're in downtown Baltimore when you get it, but that's okay. It's all by design.

We've got a camera set up across the street to catch whatever anyone else can't. The idea was never really to include news organizations enough that they could decide what our story was. Mainly, we wanted to grab their interest, and have them miss it, so they had no choice but to run our footage and our page URL when we post it.

Little Nate says it's the best way to promote Air Railroad because they have to cite the source when they show it on screen. It drives traffic, he said. It puts our name out there more. It's better, he told us, if you treat the media big boys like a delivery system, not a content creator.

Darryl wastes no time getting us to the elevator bank that goes all the way to the top. One comes almost as soon as he presses the UP button. When it dings and the doors slide open, I'm about to step in, but Darryl puts a quick hand on the box I'm carrying so two guys in suits can file out first.

"You have a good day now," he says to them as they go and they don't even nod or acknowledge he said anything.

It's perfect.

Once we're inside, Darryl swipes his card and presses the button for forty. We're going almost immediately, and it's one of those express elevators that makes my stomach lurch. In my head I have it that we'll go straight to forty with no stops in between.

That's not how it works out.

On one of the Transamerica Insurance floors, a man and a woman get on. The woman doesn't look at us, but the man stares at Darryl.

The man thinks for a moment before he says, "Aren't you supposed to be on the front desk?"

Darryl doesn't even flinch.

"Yes, sir, that's my spot, but this here is a sensitive materials delivery," Darryl says it like it's not a giant lie. "Got to be accompanied up and signed for."

"Oh," the man says, and turns around.

They get off two floors later and the man doesn't look back. I guess the answer was enough to keep him from wondering.

When the doors open on forty, I already know to veer

right and head for the stairwell with the sign that says ROOF ACCESS. It's got a heavy-looking lock on the handle and a dead bolt above it too. I'm thinking it's locked, but it's not. Darryl goes right to it, pushes it open, makes sure we're all inside, and shuts it behind us.

The second I step through I see we're not alone.

There's another man there, one landing up, staring down on us. And the worst part is, it's another security guard.

This is it right here, I think. *This is where it ends.*

55

ONLY FOR THOSE WHO LIVE TO BE FREE

This security guard, he's white with a mustache. The guy takes one look at us and coughs smoke into the air before throwing his lit cigarette to the concrete floor and kicking it out.

He starts in with, "Darryl, what in the hell—?"

He never gets to finish that sentence.

"I got love for the punctuality of your smoke break, Collins," Darryl says. "You turn off the video like usual so you don't get caught?"

As Collins just stands there looking stupid, I finally understand that this is Darryl making up for every slipup he ever made, and I'm damn grateful right then, because I know for a fact we couldn't do it without him.

"Repeat after me," Darryl says to the man. "You never saw us."

Collins has a look on his face like he doesn't want to say it, like he's about to bite his whole bottom lip off instead. But he still squeezes the words out. "I never saw you."

Darryl leads us up the stairs past Collins and when we get close, he says, "We didn't see you either."

I don't look to see if the guard reacts, or what he does next. We take steps two at a time. We blaze.

Following Darryl up the stairs as fast as we can, I watch his keys on his belt jingling and jangling, until we all stop just short of the last door and Darryl unlocks it in one swift motion, pulls, and we're out on the roof.

"Here's where you're on your own," he says. "Now go out there and show everybody that ever wondered, and ever will wonder, what Air Railroad's all about!"

Kurtis says, "Only for those who live to be free."

"For Akil," I say.

Darryl smiles, nods at us both, and like that, the door closes and he's gone.

There's no time to dwell on anything. We're out of our uniforms and tearing open boxes, jumping into our chute harnesses. Kurtis nods like a pigeon as he puts one leg through his harness and then another. I do the same. We do prechecks. I check all my straps and buckles and then I check his. He checks mine. We re-familiarize with ripcords. We double-check we're packed right. And then we do it again.

By the time we're one-hundred percent, I lean in and say, "I got a question." He nods up at me, like *bring it.*

"You're gonna jump, right?" I sniff. "I mean, lately you've been leaving the stunts up to me, and I guess it's what I've wanted, but I've been wondering why that is, why the legend was letting me take his crown awhile."

Kurtis looks at me for a second with a look like maybe I'm being ungrateful for all he's done for me, and that makes me feel guilty a little, but it doesn't make me want to know any less.

He finally says, "You good? You ready to do this?"

"I'm good," I say.

"You better be," he says, "because it's time to rise for everybody who sacrificed for you to be here. For Mon and Mike getting picked up. For Darryl putting his ass on the line. For Akil. They all made this possible. And this is *not* for nothing. Air Railroad means something. It's *got* to live on."

It sounds like there's something hiding in those last few words, the way he says them, so I call him out.

"You're sick, aren't you? Not like, got-a-cold sick. Something worse."

When my words come out and Kurtis smirks and looks away, down into the harbor, I know it's true, and what's more, I know he won't tell me. And he doesn't need to either. Too many things are clicking for me and making sense right then: how fast me and Akil got welcomed in, how Little Nate wanted to expand the brand when he did, how we rushed stunts, and most of all, it makes sense why Mon was thinking about switching from legal stuff to nursing. It's like Kurtis being for-real sick is a big old puzzle piece to everything we've been through, and it makes it all fit together in a way that feels heavy and true.

"Sorry," he says without looking me in the eye. "Sorry for making moves I wasn't always telling you about. I'm not sorry for leaning on you, though, because you're special. You deserved your shot. But I just had to make sure we leave something good behind."

My aunt's words come out of my mouth then. "Even if it kills us?"

He eyes me then, and something passes between us. Something quick and strong. Something like, *everybody's got to die sometime, right? It might as well be for what you believe in.* He smiles when he sees me feel it.

"I'll see you at the bottom," Kurtis says as he's backing up, spreading his hands out like he rests his case before turning and jogging away. "You're gonna make it. No doubt."

There's nothing else to say and I know it.

Kurtis leaves me standing there with just the plan between me and the streets below and it's as simple as it gets: We go at the same time. He's on southeast, toward Inner Harbor. I'm on southwest, toward the convention center. We go at the exact same time. They can't catch both of us.

I pull myself up onto the top lip of the roof. It's about four foot wide and concrete. Nearby me are aerials and satellite dishes. And I look down.

It's not every day you stand on top of a building.

I take it in. The people walking below with no idea I'm up here.

And then I look up. The sky is still grey. Me and it are in this together.

That gets me thinking how far I've come, how crazy life is. To go from Colorado Springs to the top of the tallest building in Baltimore in a matter of months. And I soak in that as thoughts come too fast. They smash into each other and pile up. How tall this building is. How quiet it is up here. How cold. But I think about Akil the most. How much I miss him. How he should've been here. And how nothing else matters now. Not flags or websites. Only this. Only jumping.

I'm shivering now. Not because of the cold, though. Because the adrenaline's worked its way through me, as deep as it'll go, and now I just need to go. I need to jump or I never will.

So I look to the other corner of the roof, the one pointing to the harbor on Light and Pratt, and I see Kurtis there, perched on that edge too. He's looking down. Below him, I don't see individual people, but I see a crowd and cars and bright white TV lights for reporters doing live interviews.

They don't even know we're up here. But they will. It's everything we wanted. "Are *you* good?" I'm asking Kurtis as I'm looking at him, but the second it's out of my mouth I realize it's stupid because I know he can't hear me. He's too far away.

And I know he's not good. Not even close.

I look where he's looking and see a perimeter getting set out on Pratt from South Charles to Light Street to keep the people back, to keep cars from going through. I imagine the cops licking their chops at catching us, like some cartoon wolves down there. *Finally.* That's what they must be thinking. After all the trouble we caused, P.O.S.S.E. really did catch up.

It's this moment that Kurtis picks to meet my eye. I can't really tell, but from this distance it looks like he's frowning a little. He looks scared for the first time I've ever seen, so I mouth the words, "You ready?" at him, except I exaggerate so maybe he can see what I mean. I nod my head into it. I put a question mark on the end by putting my hands up.

He gets it.

I see his body sag as he lets all his breath go before nodding, and when he nods, I feel it in my chest like glass breaking inside of me.

Because that means it's time. And it's not like some countdown shit. There's no three-two-one.

It's just *go*.

So I don't even hesitate.

I face the convention center one more time and lean out, spreading my arms behind me as I step off the edge.

Into nothing but air.

I count one second of free fall, and then pull my big chute.

The wind grabs me by the harness and rips me upward instantly. It knocks my wind out.

It's like waking up to the world from a dead sleep, getting yanked out of the world's biggest bed.

And then the air rushes around me while I'm trying to grab as much of it with my lungs as possible.

Trying to fill them.

The first and biggest thing to worry about doesn't look like it'll be an issue at all: the traffic light on Pratt and Charles.

I'm well above it. I'll clear it easy.

My breath's coming back as I go over the intersection and a pedestrian waiting to cross points up at me, like he can't believe what he's seeing.

A man. Flying.

Beneath me, I hear someone shout, "There's another one!"

I try to turn my head to see Kurtis down the block, but I can't see that far. I see the bridge in front of me, though. And my angle's bad.

I don't so much think that, as feel it. If I don't do something, I know, I'm going to crash right into that concrete.

So I do the only thing I can.

Using the ropes on my harness, I lift myself up as high as I can. I pull at them like I'm climbing in gym class and it unbalances me a little, and ripples the chute above, but I pull my legs all the way up, as high as they'll go, and almost miss every last inch of that concrete bridge.

Almost.

The back railing catches my heels and jars me forward. Pain shoots straight up my legs. That's when I lose control.

I don't even know how fast I'm going when I hit.

Whatever speed it was, I'm going at least that when I spin

and smash my hip against a metal NO PARKING sign. I don't scream when it hits me, but I want to.

Right after, I'm down in a heap like I got dropped from the top of a high dive straight onto my belly.

And I stay there.

In a pain-heavy, overwhelmed heap. Grateful I'm not dead.

But I can't move. And I can't look up.

For some reason, when tires screech right by my head, I'm sure it's knockos, but it's the van, still with the Air Express logo on it, and the back doors open up and two pairs of hands pick me up and hustle me into the back, pulling in fistfuls of parachute so we leave nothing behind.

I hear Ellah shout from the front. "Is he even alive?" I want to say yes.

And I'm about to.

But then the guys jump in. Doors shut. And gas gets hit. Just like that, we're gone.

EPILOGUE

Ellah drives us to Virginia, far enough away where no one will recognize us, and checks all of us into a hotel just over the Maryland border. We get two rooms connected by two closing doors. One for our van, and one for Kurtis's. When we open the door to our room, I get a shock, because Aunt Blue's standing there, looking angry and worried all at once. And the weird thing is she doesn't yell or anything first. She just has me lie on the bed. I feel Aunt Blue's hands on me as she's checking to see what the damage is.

She says, "Don't think for one second that because I'm here I'm not mad at you."

It's her mom voice, all stern and strong, but it doesn't cut into me. It makes me happier than I've ever been.

I try to tell her thank you. For coming anyway. For everything.

But she shushes me right up by feeding me aspirin and sending the guys out on twelve trips for ice from the ice machine, enough to fill the whole bathtub with a couple layers for me to get on top of. She says I have to lie in it—fifteen minutes on, fifteen minutes off—for an hour, just so she can see what's going on. She can't tell anything with all the swelling. Once it's down, she'll know better.

I have to get helped in there. I can barely walk.

After an hour in that tub, I'm sitting in almost melted water, and I'm sorer than I've ever been in my life, but I can move. I even stand myself up and get out of the tub. I can put weight on both ankles, but only on my toes, because my heels hurt too much to put pressure on. As I'm drying them, I see they're already threatening to turn a deep blue under the skin.

When I've managed to get some clothes on and haul myself onto the bed, Aunt Blue puts me through all kinds of little tests. She checks my mobility, my range of motion. Ankles. Knees. Hips. She pushes into my skin with her fingertips to check for ligament damage, and it all hurts. Feeling it reminds me of how Mon fixed me up when I hurt my arm, and I'm certain she'd make a good nurse if she wanted to be one still. If it'll help Kurtis any. If he even made it.

Aunt Blue prods me out of those thoughts, though. "You're the luckiest young man in the whole history of the world. Only you could jump off a building, crash, and end up with nothing more than severe hematomas."

I say, "What are those?"

"Bruising," she says.

"That's it?" I shake my head. "It feels worse."

"Oh, it could be worse," Aunt Blue says. "A lot worse. Serves you right too. You don't like it? Don't do what you been doing. Problem solved."

She's not done checking me out, though. Aunt Blue has decided this is the time to be super thorough. She checks me all over, finding out that I've got more bruising on my shoulders too, but mild, from where the harness yanked me up. And Aunt Blue is none too happy when she sees I've had recent stitches near my elbow from when I fell off Kurtis's bike trying to ride on the concrete divider.

"Where did you get this?" She wants to know.

I tell her. She gets a big frown on her face when I let her know too, but she doesn't say anything after that except, "Rest."

o   o   o

It's three hours before a knock on the door comes. By then we're all pretty sure Kurtis didn't make it, but when Ellah checks the peephole and makes a little jump for the door handle, then we figure it's good news.

"Miss me?" Kurtis walks in and does a 360 turn for everybody to see he's in one piece, like he's fine and normal, but he looks like he's a little weak, and other than that, he doesn't even have a scratch on him. "Would have been here sooner, but we had to change rides a few times before coming out here."

I can't believe it. There he is, playing the hero still. After all this. And I almost want to press him more for not telling me what's going on up on that roof, but I keep it inside as he walks over to me lying there flat on my back in the bed and says, "You alive?"

"Sure," I say.

He nods at me, and his words are heavy when he says, "Feels good, don't it?"

Little Nate is next through the door, then Mike. They make sure it's closed and locked while Aunt Blue eyes Kurtis like she wants to tear his skin off in strips for getting me to jump, but she'll let that wait for now. She'll wait for the right moment on that one. Could be a day, could be a week, but she'll let him have it eventually.

It doesn't take much pushing to hear how Kurtis got out. He's happy to tell it. "I went off when you went off," he says to me, "and I give it that one count and pull and it pops. So far, so good. I get my parachute under control, and I'm trying to head down Light to where they're all waiting"—he nods at Mike and Little Nate—"but the wind's not letting me. It's pushing me hard to the harbor, so I have to go with it, you know?"

I know, but I don't know.

He keeps rolling, talking to me mainly. "I get thinking then that I should go down in the park. You know that one with the fountain you did a flip off of?"

I nod.

"Yeah, that one. So I don't even really have to fight the wind. I just ride with it. Let it take me where it wants, which is right down onto the grass with the easiest landing I've ever had, and I just run it out onto the redbrick walkway they got there, and I stop myself right at the damn crosswalk on Light, but on the uptown side! There I am, just standing there with a parachute still on me, fiddling with the buckles, trying to get out of it. And by this time the guys have figured out I'm not coming down the other side of Light, so they've flipped around and they're creeping up with their hazards on, half on the curb, half off and they time it so perfect because they pull right behind a bus, load me in, and that's all she wrote. Smoothest escape ever."

o   o   o

The best news arrives in the newspapers the next morning. And it's at the bottom of Page One. The Baltimore District Attorney indicted Patrolman Emmanuel Leonard for the manslaughter of Akil Williams. We talk about how it should be murder instead, but at least it's something.

We all treat that like the Internet did something right for once. Like it was the reach of the people. Democracy in action. Apparently, people even called their congressmen on account of Ellah's video.

It's no guarantee of anything, but it's progress. A step in the right direction. Still, we don't celebrate it too much because we're already busy thinking about what the next move is.

And nobody will say it, but we don't know if we can go back to Charm City. Maybe it's like Little Nate said: *We're bigger than Baltimore now.*

We know we're not stopping, though.

And we're not turning ourselves in even though we're sure knockos will be coming after us. If the laws applied equally to black, white, and grey folks like me in this country, we'd do that. We'd trust the system. But we don't. So we won't.

Maybe there's no other way to fix it. No other way to change perceptions or break ceilings than to keep flying.

For Akil first and foremost.

And for anybody that ever needed to be free more than they needed to be safe. Because the truth is the truth no matter how you tell it.

It lives. It stays the same.

And in time, it transforms the world.

Because it was two people jumping off the Transamerica this time, but maybe it's four in the next place we jump, and maybe as many as twelve the time after that. It's about solidarity now. Unity.

It's about everybody, and it doesn't even have to be buildings next time. It could be the Grand Canyon. It could be Niagara Falls.

It's not a sit-in. It's not standing around holding signs and barking through bullhorns. In this right here, you ride, you jump, and every single one is a form of protest. It's civil disobedience through action.

It's a movement through *movement*.

By putting yourself on the line, you're doing it for everybody. I'm risking my life to show others that theirs are worth something.

Because the only people capable of saving us are ourselves. Not cops. Not the government.

Us.

We got to pull our own parachutes, got to show others what we're capable of. That we can dare and do, and come back to earth and do it again. That we will push limits and be so visible that people on the outside have to wear sunglasses because we're shining so bright.

Every time we do something, we're saying we matter. We're saying we can do amazing things.

And we don't need anybody's permission. Which is why this isn't the end of anything. It's the beginning.